I STILL CALL
him lord
1 PETER 3:6

A PERSONAL JOURNEY OF
UNDERSTANDING AND OPERATING
IN THE WISDOM OF SUBMISSION

WRITTEN
BY
L. MICHELE SMITH

I Still Call Him Lord

Copyright © 2014 L. Michele Smith

Published by:
Ware Resources & Publishing

We Are A One Stop Resources and Publishing Company

For more information about Ware Resources,
visit our website:

www.wareresources.com

Interior Design by David Ware Jr.
www.waresources.com

All Rights Reserved. No part of this publication may be
reproduced, stored in a retrieval system, or transmitted,
in any form by any means--electronic, mechanical, photo-
copying, recording or otherwise---without prior written
permission.

ISBN: 978-0-9844685-8-4
LC Control No.: 2015918183

Scripture quotations are from the Holy Bible, King James
Version (Public Domain).

Acknowledgments

First, I thank God for His love, leading, purpose and power in my life. He led me to complete this work that began over 16 years ago. Just a few years ago after a prophetic word and stumbling into my writings, He began urging and prodding me on to finish this book in the face of continued diversions, distractions and discouragements. At the age of 30, coming truly to know the Lord, I realized that He created me for a specific purpose, and that continues even now to be very powerful, rewarding and meaningful for me.

Secondly, I am very thankful for my dear husband of 21 years, Andrew, whom God only blessed me with after I surrendered my life totally to Him. We have both come to love the Lord dearly and have committed our lives to God the Father of our Lord Jesus Christ, who is the center of our lives and our marriage. We learned very early before exchanging our wedding vows that marriage takes three. Without God, we would have never made it through some of the toughest and stormy challenges in our lives.

I thank my niece and friend, Pastor Loretta Butler of West End, North Carolina, for being a wonderful encouragement and prayer support. Finally, I thank God for my late parents. My father, Tom David Fuller, planted seeds in my life for worship; prayer and the song that he ministered so powerfully that touched my life, "Only Believe." My mom, Blanche Mae Fuller, watered those seeds, displaying such quiet strength, ever calmly and consistently encouraging me. I can hear it as if it was yesterday, "Michele, you have to put God first " I finally got it and later discovered this verse in scripture, "But seek ye first the kingdom of God, and His righteousness; and all these things shall be added unto you" **(Mt. 6:33)**. To God be the glory!

Introduction

This is about my journey with God yielding as a married woman to the transforming power of His word and learning the wisdom of submission. As a young girl around the age of ten, I began dreaming about having a family. This meant the world to me. I had a perfect picture of what my family would look like. There I was as a mom with the dad and the precious, neatly dressed children all smiling, appearing as though they did not have a care in the world.

How sad it was to see that picture marred and disfigured because of how the world, the flesh and the devil were all working together like an unholy trinity to dash my hopes and steal my dreams. Yet what a joy to experience the supernatural work of Christ Jesus the Lord in restoring all things.

"And they shall build the old wastes, they shall raise up the former desolations, and they shall repair the waste cities, the desolations of many generations" **(Is. 61:4).**

Fast forward, now here I am post-redemptive, married to Andrew, God's man for me, my hardworking, handsome, intelligent husband, and we have our bright, gifted and talented children. So what now? The happy ending you see on TV, right? Not quite, let's push that "THE END" sign out of the way.

Thus began my journey of faith in the important, lifelong process of becoming a living testimony not only before the world, with my wallet full of snap shots of the family and the dog, but also behind the scenes in the private household of the Smith family. Welcome, come on in, as I share with you what the Teacher, The Holy Spirit began to teach me about how to be a victorious woman of God.

Early in our marriage, God introduced to me the concept of submission, and believe me, I was horrified at the thought of it. Not that my husband was a bad person; No, look at it like this. You have been on your own and are used to driving yourself around. You have worked and figured out how to get from point A to point B, having begun to master the art of daily living, and suddenly someone says, "I need you to move over because someone else has to drive now."(Repositioning).

Can you see this picture? Just a simple scenario of the unique positioning in God's Word and His design for family life.

"For the husband is head of the wife, even as Christ is the head of the church: and he is the savior of the body"**(Eph. 5:23)**.

So about two years into our marriage, I began to consistently hear the gentle voice of the Spirit saying, "Sarah's daughters." I heard it so much it irritated me, and I responded aloud, "OK, what is *'Sarah's daughters?'*" It was then very apparent to me that God was speaking and that I needed to humble my little self and pay attention.

"But I don't even know that much about Sarah," I said. I knew the basics: She was married to Abraham, the father of faith, and she gave birth to a child when she was past childbearing age. I think that's all I knew about her.

After I had begun to search the scriptures and study, I was surprised and amazed at how much the Bible mentions her. I found as I studied her and the concept of submission that she is a wonderful model, and through her, God provides great principles for teaching married women. Little did I know how God in His merciful kindness was equipping me to go through some of the most challenging times in my marriage.

"For after this manner in the old time the holy women also, who trusted in God, adorned themselves, being in subjection unto their own husbands: "Even as Sarah obeyed Abraham, calling him lord: whose daughters ye are, as long as ye do well, and are not afraid with any amazement"**(1 Pet. 3:5-6)**.

Through Sarah's life and those of many holy women of old, I would learn and share with others in my home meeting/care group. *(You can guess what I called this ministry.)* I shared this so that I and others like the holy women could go through the storms that come in this world and emerge victorious in Jesus Christ.

Several times, God brought precious people into our lives in the course of the day, giving me and Andrew opportunities to listen, encourage and share. Often, Andrew would have me on one end with the wife while, he was on the other end with the husband. How amazed I was when some time later we would find out they were a married couple. This was the Lord validating that as He helped us and we remained open to it, that He also wanted us to help others.

Table Of Contents

Who Is Sarah? 1

What Is Submission? 10

In Harm's Way 22

Women In Intercession 38

You Are Going to Have This Baby! 56

God's Command to the Husband 67

God's Command to the Wife 71

Divided Devotions? 78

Calling him "Lord" 87

Who is Sarah?

So began my journey of obedience to God and the transformation power of His word. As I listened, he began teaching and mentoring me through Sarah's life into becoming a daughter of God. The Lord was moving me from my old mindset and stunted belief that there was not much in the Bible about Sarah, other than her being Abraham's wife and giving birth to the miracle baby Isaac she conceived past the time of fertility for women.

I read from **Genesis 11:27** through **24:67** finding that not only did the Bible speak of her being the wife of Abraham, the father of faith, but it also addressed her barrenness, her extraordinary beauty and her anguish while waiting for her desire to bear a child to be fulfilled. The Bible also addressed her fears and her failure when she tried to help God fulfill the promise of a son through her Egyptian handmaid, Hagar, in **Genesis 16.**

"And Abram and Nahor took them wives: the name of Abram's wife was Sarai; and the name of Nahor's wife, Milcah, the daughter of Haran, the father of Milcah, and the father of Iscah. But Sarai was barren; he had no child" **(Gen. 11:29-30).**

It also speaks of her courage and the favor of God over her life as she submitted to her husband, Abraham, when he was fearful and not doing the best job at following the Lord or being her husband **(Gen. 12:11-14).**

"And it came to pass, when he was come near to enter into Egypt, that he said unto Sarai his wife, Behold now, I know that thou art a fair woman to look upon: Therefore it shall come to pass, when the Egyptians shall see thee, that they shall say, This is his wife: and they will kill me, but they will save thee alive. Say, I pray thee, thou art my sister: that it may be well with me for thy sake; and my soul shall live because of thee"**(Gen. 12:11-13).**

"And he entreated Abram well for her sake..."**(Gen. 12:16).**

Sarah is referenced in **Isaiah 51:2** where followers of Jesus Christ are admonished to look to her as well as Abraham, "Look unto Abraham your father, and unto Sarah that bare you...."

We can endeavor to gain a greater understanding of the reason why

Who is Sarah?

the Lord would instruct us this way. One important reason is that we would understand the sufferings of Christ from looking to Sarah in the way of faith in submission, and the anguish experienced as noted in **Isaiah 54:1,** waiting for the promise to have a son.

God spoke prophetic words over her life, "And I will bless her, and give thee a son also of her: yea, I will bless her, and she shall be a mother of nations; kings of people shall be of her" **(Gen. 17:16)**. He declared when she wasn't even pregnant, and we can learn from this; He waited until she was beyond the years of child bearing, when it looked completely impossible.

I call this intense place *The Process* of faith when one receives a word or promise from the Lord to its manifest fulfillment; in other words, the waiting period that comes between conception and the tangible manifestation of a promise from God.

Another example, speaking of holy women of old is Hannah in the temple **1 Samuel 1:8-12**; we find her travailing in prayer and going as far as making a vow to give the child she desired so much back to the Lord all the days of his life if He would give her this experience. The Apostle Paul used this same kind of laboring language *(birthing)* in **Galatians 4:19** as he referred to the travail, *The Process* or the faith work of producing sons of God: "My little children of whom I travail in birth again until Christ be formed in you...."

Another important learning tip is that there is a price to living out and laying hold of the benefits of the kingdom and the promises of God. The Bible talks about it in **Matthew 11** when Jesus is testifying about John the Baptist ... *(my view and paraphrase)*. The eternal blessings of the kingdom of God calls for a believer to have a good and stable relationship with the Lord, strong resolve, and an attitude of violence, violent faith. To put it an- other way, a very popular phrase I've heard is that the promises of God are not automatic!

James 2:14-26 addresses this very truth as he writes about faith and deeds; "What doth it profit, my brethren, though a man say he hath faith, and have not works? can faith save him?...."

We really need to get this because very often this is missed by believ- ers who have learned to cloak things in religiosity and popular clichés, but have no real faith action.

There is a price, not for salvation. No, Jesus Christ the only begotten Son of God paid that price in full by His blood on the cross at Calvary, yet also for so much more if you really want to embrace all He has intended for you to have in the way of the more abundant life **(Jn. 10:10)**, you must understand this.

Therefore, whether you have received a prophetic word or a promise, you must have a strong resolve and determination that says failure and defeat are not an option for the thing for which you believe God. Nothing or no one should be able to persuade you otherwise once you have settled that in your heart and can honestly say, *"I have talked with the Lord and spent time in His word. I've waited in His presence and gotten His nod of approval, the Yes and Amen on this. The scepter of righteousness has been extended to me"* **(Es. 8:4; Mt. 6:33; Heb. 1:8)**.

Next in the process of faith is the work that comes as you walk by faith or your faith actions:

"Enlarge the place of thy tent, and let them stretch forth the curtains of thine habitations: spare not, lengthen thy cords, and strengthen thy stakes" (**Is. 54:2**).

Remember Noah, he probably looked pretty ridiculous **(Gen. 6:13-22)**.

Now, some may not like to hear this, but there is warfare as you move toward your miracle, moving in faith and this is serious: Apostle Paul speak-ing: "This charge I commit unto thee, son Timothy, according to the proph-ecies which went before on thee, that thou by them mightiest war a good warfare"**(1 Tim. 1:18)**.

The next verse warns us of the outcome of neglecting this: "Holding faith, and a good conscience; which some having put away concerning faith have made shipwreck" **(1 Tim. 1:19)**.

Here the Bible gives an example of the travail *(labor or work)* of the soul which through faith actions touch the heart of God and brings about His powerful results through Hannah.

Who is Sarah?

"Why are you crying, Hannah?" Elkanah would ask. "Why aren't you eating? Why be downhearted just because you have no children? You have me. Isn't that better than having ten sons?" Once after a sacrificial meal at Shiloh, Hannah got up and went to pray. Eli the priest was sitting at his customary place beside the entrance of the Tabernacle.

Hannah was in deep anguish, crying bitterly as she prayed **(I Sam. 1:8-12).** Eli the priest thought she was drunk **(I Sam. 1:13).**

In the New Testament, the Apostle Paul also was called to suffer greatly for the cause of Christ **(Acts 9:16 and Gal. 4:19).** Encouraging the believers, Paul writes, "...work out your own salvation with fear and trembling **(Phil. 2:12).**

In the words of Jesus Himself regarding the warfare: "And from the days of John the Baptist until now the kingdom of heaven suffereth violence, and the violent take it by force" **(Mt. 11:12).** My discovery of the working process of a word or promise from God carried through to fruition, through studying or looking to Sarah has given me a battle stance against the enemies of God *(the world, the flesh and the devil)* and a strong resolve to the pursuit of my purpose and destiny in Him.

"For I know the thoughts that I think toward you, saith the Lord, thoughts of peace, and not of evil, to give you an expected end"**(Jer. 29:11).**

This also moves me to serve in the encouragement of the purpose and destiny of others, as an intercessor and helper. I thank God that He is faithful in strengthening us as women, wives in particular with how to go through and get through, yet remain joyful going from one level of victory to the next for the seasons that come in our lives, families, our world today and ministry life in the Kingdom of God. Jesus said we would have trouble here: "...In the world ye shall have tribulation *(trouble)*: but be of good cheer, I have overcome the world"**(Jn. 16:33).**

He reminded us that he came to give us a more abundant life **(Jn. 10:10).**

Once I asked God literally to please show me how to be of good cheer. I was hurting, but did not want to do anything that would displease the Lord; and He did giving me this word.

"Rejoicing in hope, patient in tribulation *(trouble)*, continuing instant in prayer" **(Rom. 12:12).**

There are periods of suffering and challenges as we live in this world and in this flesh; yet there is an adventurous journey of transformation through the word of God for us as married women.

Looking to Sarah and one another who are her daughters at various points in of the process, let's be thankful as we get fresh encouragement of wisdom and revelation in studying, learning and growing all because our awesome and loving Heavenly Father has already guaranteed us a victorious and fulfilled life. Consider the price He paid for this to be so!

I've come to realize that the things I desire, more often than not God wants for me more than I do, just as we want good things for our children and make great sacrifices for them to have them. The glorious, eternal life of pleasures and fullness of joy lost through sin Jesus has redeemed for us by His blood **(Rev. 12:11).**

With this understanding that warfare comes with the territory, may we ever be inclined to cooperate with the Holy Spirit's work of developing us to the glory of the Father, the glory that fills the earth, Christ in us the hope of glory *(paraphrased)* **(Col. 1:27),** Hallelujah!

"And one cried unto another, and said, Holy, holy, holy, is the Lord of hosts: the whole earth is full of his glory" **(Is. 6:3).**

In Christ, we come to realize that we are a part of this awesome visual.

No longer should a thief be allowed just to come up in our homes unopposed. Whether I am so sweetly in the kitchen cooking dinner or baking cookies, out shopping or jostling for promotion and status in the corporate world, no longer do I allow the devil just to come up in my family. Instead, now with greater revelation, I do all these things fully clothed in the battle array of Jesus with the help of the Holy Spirit.

"Put on the whole armour of God, that ye may be able to stand against the wiles of the devil" **(Eph. 6:11).**

I am anointed and baking those cookies, anointed as I am out shopping and even as I am vying for promotion in the corporate world if that's in God's plan for me. Hallelujah, to God be the glory!

Who is Sarah?

"Praying always with all prayer and supplication in the Spirit, and watching thereunto with all perseverance and supplication for all saints" **(Eph. 6:18).**

Submission is an adornment, something to put on and to be worn just like the armor in **Ephesians 6.** It's not recognized just as the outward spiritual gear we put on but also as the inner man, "the hidden man of the heart" **(1 Pet. 3:4).**

This is very significant for battle. This gentle and quiet spirit, free from the grip of fear, is less prone to fleshy, carnal reaction. It is not so much in the word spoken but more of what's demonstrated in behavior and attitude. **Proverbs 25:15** says, "By long forbearing is a prince persuaded, and a soft tongue breaketh the bone."

It is a costly adorning, very precious to God as He looks on, seeing us so grounded in faith, helping one another as much as we're able. Jesus was submitted to the Father, so this is not just a concept for women but men also, all believers.

It's just pointed out here in the part or the role of married women to help us have a clear definition, to be distinct in our part in this world and to be powerful in the Lord. The devil hates marriage because it is really pointing to something greater. It's about Christ and the church **(Eph. 5:32).** If we can just get the picture, it holds the great possibility of lives saved for Jesus. That's the ultimate mission here on earth in the Lord that we want to get under (sub = meaning under).

John said it very well in **John 3:30**, "He must increase, but I must decrease."

Sarah is a mentor for married women, but also for the unmarried as we move forward in pursuing and carrying out the faith of God, discovering and embracing God's greater purpose for us, the purpose for which we were created. Then, we give no place to fear even though we may feel shaken by everything around us that says, "This can't be." We stand firm believing for the promise of God in Jesus that is Yes and Amen, now that's powerful!

"...for more are the children of the desolate than the children of the married wife, saith the Lord" **(Is.54:1).**

Hear this now, because Sarah was married but desolate; meaning isolated, abandoned, forsaken. I wondered why God used Sarah and why He used Abraham in referring to one not obeying the word in (**1 Peter 3:1),** "Likewise, ye wives, be in subjection to your own husbands; that, if any obey not the word, they also may without the word be won by the conversation of the wives."

I believe it's for us to see them as being just as human as we are, with our own weaknesses and to have hope as He points us all to The Husband Jesus. "For thy Maker is thine husband..."**(Is. 54:5).**

This is in no way to undermine our natural husbands, or to undermine women with dreams and desires, married or unmarried. On the contrary, it helps and enhances everything; it reminds and speaks to every one of us that it's about Him. It gets us out of the way and prepares a platform where God gets to display His glory, that is the ultimate end all, that God stands alone as God, because He is, and our giving Him praise because He's good.

Models

In the beginning when God created the heaven and the earth, we have our models whom God made to be like Him in **Genesis 1**, Adam and Eve who had everything perfect and fouled up, as we do, *paraphrased* **(Genesis 3)**. Later in **Genesis 18** and **Isaiah 51:2** we have our models Abraham and Sarah through whom would come the promised child Isaac, so little Isaac was a model too. Abraham demonstrates hope in God that stood in the face of hopelessness, rejoicing as he believed what God said.

1 Pet. 3:1-2 encourages married women through the life of Sarah to be a model before their husbands by submission, without the word. As a model walks the runway, she doesn't talk, she models. OK ladies, lets hit the runway and walk by faith, trusting Him and experiencing the rewards of God, **(Heb. 11:6)** knowing when to speak and when to take action.

When you begin talking about following God in this way, people will think you are foolish, drunk or worse. Just remember the foolishness of God is wiser than men, so how much more is the supreme wisdom of God.

Who is Sarah?

When it all comes together, everyone in their part, we get the excellence of the power of Christ and the awesome love of God flowing, and that's astounding. Love is who God is, and He never fails, and when we are in His love, as obedient followers we won't fail either.

So, Who is Sarah?(summary)
She is the freewoman, found in **Galatians 4:22-31:**

22 For it is written, that Abraham had two sons, the one by a bondmaid, the other by a freewoman.

23 But he who was of the bondwoman was born after the flesh; but he of the freewoman was by promise.

24 Which things are an allegory: for these are the two covenants; the one from the mount Sinai, which gendereth to bondage, which is Agar.

25 For this Agar is Mount Sinai in Arabia, and answereth to Jerusalem which now is, and is in bondage with her children.

26 But Jerusalem which is above is free, which is the mother of us all.

27 For it is written, Rejoice, thou barren that bearest not; break forth and cry, thou that travailest not: for the desolate hath many more children than she which hath a husband.

28 Now we, brethren, as Isaac was, are the children of promise.

29 But as then he that was born after the flesh persecuted him that was born after the Spirit, even so it is now.

30 Nevertheless what saith the scripture? Cast out the bondwoman and her son: for the son of the bondwoman shall not be heir with the son of the freewoman.

31 So then, brethren, we are not children of the bondwoman, but of the free.

The way of flesh *(natural, ordinary, man's way or carnal)* is contrary to the way of the Spirit of Christ. One represents bondage and the other freedom. *She is a woman of faith*, found in **Hebrews** what some call the Hall of Faith," Through faith also Sara herself received strength to conceive seed, and was delivered of a child when she was past age, because she judged him faithful who had promised "**(Heb. 11:11).**

She is barren, found in **Romans 4:19,** "and being not weak in faith, he considered not his own body now dead, when he was about a hundred years old, neither yet the deadness of Sarah's womb."

This is to encourage our faith, whatever our weakness or deficiency may be that limits us and prevents us from having the satisfied and fulfilled life that Jesus promises in **John 10:10.**

She is a model to her husband, found in **1 Peter 3:1-6:** "...they also may without the word be won by the conversation of the wives." Your godly lives will speak to them without any words. They will be won over by observing your pure and reverent lives. This is how the holy women of old made themselves beautiful. Sara stands with other holy women of old.

She possessed not only natural beauty but also spiritual beauty. **1 Peter 3:3-4.**

She is a model for other married women, In **1 Peter 3:6,** she learned how to walk in an excellent spirit favored of God in the midst of danger when her husband was in fear amidst a struggle of faith and obedience in his life. "Even as Sara obeyed Abraham, calling him lord: whose daughters ye are, as long as ye do well, and are not afraid with any amazement."

She is the only woman noted in the Bible whose name is changed by God, **Genesis 17:15** "And God said unto Abraham, As for Sarai thy wife, thou shalt not call her name Sarai, but Sarah shall her name be."

What Is Submission?

Proverbs 4:7 says, "Wisdom is the principal thing; therefore get wisdom: and with all thy getting get understanding."

Getting a fresh definition of submission was a very important start to my journey of growth as a believing wife trying to understand what God was saying. Though saved for many years and loving the Lord, I still had a mindset influenced by world views of important matters like marriage, family and other life issues that were off and incorrect. The following things were very important for study to renew my mind. Simply put, God's way is true and right, and reviewing basic definitions of submission from the perspective of Truth(the Bible), though hard at first and somewhat constricting, led to greater freedom and effectiveness for our good and the praise and purpose of God.

What Does the Word "Submission" Mean?

Source: Dictionary.com. Collins English Dictionary - Complete & Un-abridged 10th Edition.HarperCollins Publishers.http://dictionary. reference. com/browse/submission

Basic definition:

1. *An act or instance of submitting*
2. *The condition of having submitted*
3. *Submissive conduct or attitude*

Synonyms – *appeasement, bowing down, cringing, giving in, humbleness, humility, obedience*

Antonyms – *fight, resistance*

History origin, submission early 15c act of referring to a third party for judgment or decision; a lowering, reduce yield

Topical Index definition

Humble obedience to another's will Strong's

dictionary of Bible words says:

What is Submission?

Hebrew/Aramaic
anah (1) to afflict, be afflicted
raphac (1) to trample, to prostrate – humble self Greek

What is Submission? *hupeuko (1) to surrender, yield, submit self hupotasso*
(6) subordinate: to obey

From The Bible – To Whom It Applies

Let's follow the word – submission, subject, obedient…

All of Us –"Submitting yourselves one to another in the fear of God"**(Eph.5:21).**

Wives–"Wives, submit yourselves unto your own husbands, as unto the Lord"**(Eph. 5:22).**

Children – "Children, obey your parents in the Lord, for this is right. Honour your father and mother; which is the first commandment with promise; that it may be well with thee, and thou mayest live long on the earth"**(Eph. 6:1-3).**

Rulers–"Submit yourselves to every ordinance of man for the Lord's sake: whether it be to the king as supreme;… For so is the will of God, that with well doing ye may put to silence the ignorance of foolish men:" **(1 Pet. 2:13,15):**

Business – "Servants, be subject to your masters with all fear; not only to the good and gentle, but also to the froward. For this is thank worthy, if a man for conscience toward God endure grief, suffering wrongfully" **(1 Pet. 2:18-19).**

Elders –"Likewise, ye younger, submit yourselves unto your elder. Yea, all of you be subject to one another, and be clothed with humility; for God resisteth the proud, and giveth grace to the humble"**(1 Pet. 5:5).**

Christian Leaders –"Obey them that have the rule over you, and submit yourselves: for they watch for your souls, as they that must give account, that they may do it with joy, and not with grief: for that is unprofitable for you"**(Heb. 13:17).**

To God – "Submit yourselves therefore to God. Resist the devil, and he will flee from you"**(Jas. 4:7).**

So, whatever our role(s) as believers, we are instructed to do all as unto the Lord by the word of God **(Col. 3:17).**

"And whatsoever ye do in word or deed, do all in the name of the Lord Jesus, giving thanks to God and the Father by him."

Examples From the Bible

Breakthrough and answered prayer are obtained when submission is embraced and acted upon. This is like hidden treasure that unlocks blessings, favor and power that everybody doesn't get to experience.

The Centurion's submission for his servant and to Jesus (Mat. 8:5-10):

5. And when Jesus was entered into Capernaum, there came unto him a centurion, beseeching him,

6. And saying, Lord, my servant lieth at home sick of the palsy, grievously tormented.

7. And Jesus saith unto him, I will come and heal him.

8 The centurion answered and said, Lord, I am not worthy that thou shouldest come under my roof: but speak the word only, and my servant shall be healed.

9 For I am a man under authority, having soldiers under me: and I say to this man, Go, and he goeth; and to another, Come, and he cometh; and to my servant, Do this, and he doeth it.

10 When Jesus heard it, he marvelled, and said to them that followed, Verily I say unto you, I have not found so great faith, no, not in Israel.

What is Submission?

The Shunem woman's submission to her husband

A powerful story of faith. She is the women spoken of in Hebrews 11:35 who received their dead back to life **(2 Kgs 4:9-10, 22-23).**

9 And she said unto her husband, Behold now, I perceive that this is a holy man of God, which passeth by us continually.

10 Let us make a little chamber, I pray thee, on the wall; and let us set for him there a bed, and a table, and a stool, and a candlestick: and it shall be, when he cometh to us, that he shall turn in thither.

22 And she called unto her husband, and said, Send me, I pray thee, one of the young men, and one of the asses, that I may run to the man of God, and come again.

23 And he said, Wherefore wilt thou go to him today? it is neither new moon, nor sabbath. And she said, It shall be well.

Sarah's submission to Abraham

She is another woman mentioned and named for her faith in Hebrews 11:11, "Hall of Faith"

Gen. 12:11-16

11 And it came to pass, when he was come near to enter into Egypt, that he said unto Sarai his wife, Behold now, I know that thou art a fair woman to look upon:

12 Therefore it shall come to pass, when the Egyptians shall see thee, that they shall say, This is his wife: and they will kill me, but they will save thee alive.

13 Say, I pray thee, thou art my sister: that it may be well with me for thy sake; and my soul shall live because of thee.

13

14 And it came to pass, that, when Abram was come into Egypt, the Egyptians beheld the woman that she was very fair.

15 The princes also of Pharaoh saw her, and commended her before Pharaoh: and the woman was taken into Pharaoh's house.

16 And he entreated Abram well for her sake: and he had sheep, and oxen, and he asses, and menservants, and maidservants, and she asses, and camels.

I'll share more about this powerful story in the next chapter.

Jesus' submission to his earthly parents
We have this story about Jesus visiting the temple with his parents and re- maining behind so that they had to return to search for him **(Lk. 2:48-51).**

"And when they saw him, they were amazed: and his mother said unto him, why hast thou thus dealt with us? behold, thy father and I have sought thee sorrowing. And he said unto them, How is it that ye sought me? wist ye not that I must be about my Father's business? And they understood not the saying which he spake unto them. And he went down with them, and came to Nazareth, and was subject unto them: but his mother kept all these sayings in her heart."

A Testimony

I brought a heartfelt concern to the Lord about our youngest child, Maile Anna, who at the time was 12 years old about to turn 13. I was just dreading the whole teenager crazy age *(my fourth one)*. He began leading me to pray in this manner, as the scripture above regarding my daughter's development. I am so grateful for the Lord's direction, and His help with how to pray according to His Word over her life, His will. Praying prophetically, it just came right to me, and I felt encouraged and empowered by the Holy Spirit to continue to pray, teach and speak the power of His word over her life regarding submission.

What is Submission?

I so appreciate that fact that God will partner with us in raising our children if we ask Him. As I think again, it's really we who are partnering with Him for His intent and purpose for the children He has entrusted to us.

Do you love Me? ...Feed My sheep

"He saith unto him the third time, Simon, son of Jonas, lovest thou me? Peter was grieved because he said unto him the third time, Lovest thou me? And he said unto him, Lord, thou knowest all things; thou knowest that I love thee. Jesus saith unto him, Feed my sheep"**(Jn. 21:17)**.

I have found when listening in on break room conversations, "downtime" sharing and other social settings that many parents have similar concerns and are often not sure of what to do with their children during the teen years. When we're not sure it's easy to become afraid. Some parents become afraid of their children, afraid of not being their child's best friend or of somehow losing their love, as well as afraid for them.

The Bible clearly teaches that we are to require obedience from our children and remain firm and consistent about it because we are accountable to God and will have to answer to Him **(1 Sam. 2:27-30)**. The encouragement from my own experience is to know that our Father God is there to listen to us when we have concerns about our children and to help when we ask. We have to trust Him over our fears and obey Him when He tells us what to do, just as Abraham did. "By faith Abraham, when he was tried, offered up Isaac: and he that had received the promises offered up his only begotten son," It may feel scary sometimes but just remember that God loves our children much more than we ever can and He loves us too" **(Heb. 11:17)**.

Christ's submission to the Father

"And he went a little farther, and fell on His face, and prayed, saying, O my Father, if it be possible, let this cup pass from me: nevertheless not as I will, but as thou wilt"**(Mt. 26:39)**.

"He went away again the second time, and prayed, saying, O my Father, if this cup may not pass away from me, except I drink it, thy will be done" **(Mt. 26:42).**

Following Christ Requires Submission To Him

"And whosoever doth not bear his cross, and come after me, cannot be my disciple." … **Lk. 14:27).**

Now, this is very straightforward and can be hard to hear, because we may feel that we're not ready, that we are incapable of doing it consistently and sincerely, or, maybe we have just a little too much pride, thinking we're already OK. That's what so awesome about God. He's merciful, gracious, long suffering, and always abundant in goodness and truth. We just have to stay honest before Him. I know He waited a long time for me to get to submission. He was patient and allowed me time on my own to foul things up enough, until I was just disgusted with myself, fed up with failure and defeat while doing things my own way. God understands, and I have learned that the development of godly character and maturity as a believer in the Lord Jesus Christ is a process.

Luke 14:28 reminds us to count the cost before we begin a task. We do need to think seriously and soberly about our commitment to the things of God and His Kingdom and not take them lightly. Remember, we are ambassadors, and God has given us the Gift, the Holy Spirit to be with us forever and to help us. We just need to stay humble and honest before the Lord. He is a loving Father, not like some of us who through world views have adopted a disposable mentality and will quickly throw out the baby with the bath water when things don't appear to be perfect. (*Ask me how I know, because I was ready to throw myself out.*

Great fractures and regret come because we, like those disciples, hear of God's hard requirements and too quickly decide to walk away. **(Jn. 6:50-66)** "This is the bread which cometh down from heaven, that a man may eat thereof, and not die....." In Verse 66, it says, "From that time

What is Submission?

many of his disciples went back, and walked no more with him." The undeniable failure of marriage is evident in the horrifying statistics we have today, even in marriages among believers!Families are torn apart, absolutely devastated because many of us do not connect the cross that the Lord tells us to take up every day and follow Him in our home relationships and family life, *paraphrased* **(Lk. 9:23).**

We hesitate to trust God and fear the suffering that comes with the territory of submission, and it's understandable. It is hard and the cost can just seem too high to pay, but I believe our best training ground for ministry begins in our own households. If we would only with grateful hearts discipline our- selves to remember Jesus when those hard times hit and reflect on the price He paid to save undeserving humanity you and me. Jesus says come to Him, He will destroy that yoke and remove the burden weighing you down, *paraphrased* **(Mt. 11:28-30).** Thank God that Jesus didn't quit before He completed the gruesome work of the cross of Calvary but humbly submitted to God. He didn't want to go through either. Though it looked bad for Jesus when He was beaten beyond human recognition and hanging on that cross, what was really happening was a divine set up for the greatest victory ever wrought in all of creation, our redemption! And so through our humble submission to Christ in everything, great victories will continue to be manifested to the world.

"Verily, verily, I say unto you, He that believeth on me, the works that I do shall he do also; and greater works than these shall he do; because I go unto my Father"**(Jn. 14:12).**

Learning to Submit

"But I would have you know, that the head of every man is Christ; and the head of the woman is the man; and the head of Christ is God" **(1 Cor. 11:3).**

"For the man is not of the woman: but the woman of the man. Neither was the man created for the woman; but the woman for the man **(1 Cor. 11:8-9).**

"Nevertheless neither is the man without the woman, neither the woman without the man, in the Lord. For as the woman is of the man, even so is the man also by the woman; but all things of God" **(1 Cor. 11:11-12).**

A life submitted to Christ is a life lived by the Spirit and not the flesh *(the very seat of our will, emotions and intellect)*, and will ultimately bring glory to God. "This I say then, Walk in the Spirit, and ye shall not fulfill the lust of the flesh **(Gal. 5:16).**

Marriage requires mutual submission: Eph. 5: 21-33

21 Submitting yourselves one to another in the fear of God.

22 Wives, submit yourselves unto your own husbands, as unto the Lord.

23 For the husband is the head of the wife, even as Christ is the head of the church: and he is the saviour of the body.

24 Therefore as the church is subject unto Christ, so let the wives be to their own husbands in every thing.

25 Husbands, love your wives, even as Christ also loved the church, and gave himself for it;

26 That he might sanctify and cleanse it with the washing of water by the word,

27 That he might present it to himself a glorious church, not having spot, or wrinkle, or any such thing; but that it should be holy and without blemish.

28 So ought men to love their wives as their own bodies. He that loveth his wife loveth himself.

29 For no man ever yet hated his own flesh; but nourisheth and cherisheth it, even as the Lord the church:

30 For we are members of his body, of his flesh, and of his bones

What is Submission?

31 For this cause shall a man leave his father and mother, and shall be joined unto his wife, and they two shall be one flesh

32 This is a great mystery: but I speak concerning Christ and the church.

33 Nevertheless let every one of you in particular so love his wife even as himself; and the wife see that she reverence her husband.

The Bigger Picture, Common Purpose

Apostle Paul inspired by the Spirit of God says that the relationship of marriage tells a great mystery, and that mystery is Christ and the church **(Eph. 5:32)**. The marriage relationship is to be held in highest regard in this natural life than all others, according to **Hebrews 13:4.** It says, "Marriage is honourable in all, and the bed undefiled: but whore mongers and adulterers God will judge." Through this particular relationship, God desires to model or present a picture to the world of His relationship to the church to which all are invited to be a part. It is also a temporal thing in the order of this world that will not continue in the life that is to come, eternal life **(Mk. 12:25)**. "For when they shall rise from the dead, they neither marry, nor are given in marriage; but are as the angels which are in heaven."

These things far surpass what we are able to see or comprehend in our human minds. No wonder marriage is under such constant attack. God still desires to show us and to ignite our faith through pertinent earthly things, heavenly mysteries to bring us into an understanding of what He has prepared for those who love Him. This can never be fully realized through lives unwilling to submit.

"If I have told you earthly things, and ye believe not, how shall ye believe, if I tell you of heavenly things" **(Jn. 3:12)**?

Know, precious daughters, Gods requires us to model before our own husbands our life of faith in Him through submission, whether they are obedient or disobedient to the Word of God **(1 Pet. 3:1-2)**. He has woven our role

19

as wives into the fabric of His church building work.

"Every wise woman buildeth her house: but the foolish plucketh it down with her hands"**(Prov. 14:1).**

He has endowed us with such powerful influence in our households and the devil recognizes it, as he did when the serpent tempted Eve **(Gen. 3:1).** That is why the warfare gets so intense between Satan and each woman living to serve God *(We are symbolic of the church)*. This started back before time **(Rev. 12)** and continues on today, so it really is not about us. Thank God the fight has been fought and the victory won through Jesus Christ our Lord.

"But thanks be to God, which giveth us the victory through our Lord Jesus Christ"**(I Cor. 15:57).**

Let me tell you a secret, *it's ours,* all of ours! That is certainly reason to give God praise. So, it is very important for us to choose our battles wisely and get past petty differences *(which can be used demonically as hindrances and distractions)* and to pour out genuine love *(agape)* on one another. We all need that caring embrace, a word or just a smile to get us through hardships that come to all, while we still have to be strong, patient, sober and vigilant in this world "because our adversary the devil, as a roaring lion, walketh about, seeking whom he may devour" **(I Pet. 5:8).** Then we can stand ready to fight for one another with our powerful weapons of Go **(Eph. 6:10-18)** loving, serving and praying.

Now, pardon my forwardness in this, but when I talk about prayer I'm not talking about mamsy-pamsy prayers when we're dealing with a fierce enemy that wants to destroy, and not the kind in which we're praying the problem instead of the answer.

What is Submission?

I am talking about the effective, unrelenting and fiery kind of prayer loaded with the word of God, fueled by the love of God that get answers, intercession that gives birth to results! I'll share more about that too in a later chapter. Yet as empowered as we are through Christ, it all starts with submitted life.

So What Does It Mean?

"Sub – mission" is a compound word that means to come under (sub and to carry out to completion a specific assignment (mission). *It is for everyone. For me, learning my role as a wife was what God was impressing upon me. The reward is realizing that as I yield to God in everything, He shows Himself strong for me, and it makes it easier for others around me to do the same.*

Submission is the key to living the full, more abundant life God promised **(Jn. 10:10).**

Jesus made a profound statement in response to the faith of the centurion who came to Him on behalf of his servant. The centurion could operate in this kind of faith because he had an understanding of submission.

"When Jesus heard it, He marvelled, and said to those who followed, Verily I say unto you, I have not found so great faith, no, not in Israel. And I say unto you, that many shall come from the east and west, and shall sit down with Abraham, and Isaac, and Jacob, in the kingdom of heaven. But the children of the kingdom shall be cast out into outer darkness: there shall be weeping and gnashing of teeth" **(Matthew 8:10-12).**

So not only is submission important to understand, but it also is serious and worth taking another look.

In Harm's Way

In no way am I suggesting that women follow along and submit to their husbands or anyone if there is a real threat to their lives, their children's lives or even to their husband's lives. I believe getting wisdom, being connected to a healthy church and having a good support system is vital **(Prv. 4:5; Heb. 10:25; Jm. 5:16).**

When separation from a spouse occurs, which indeed at times is absolutely necessary, it should be done prayerfully with a goal and plan in place that is well communicated to each person so that the family can be healed, reconciled and reunited stronger than ever.

"Even as Sara obeyed Abraham, calling him lord: whose daughters ye are, as long as ye do well, and are not afraid with any amazement"**(1 Pet. 3:6).**

In this chapter, we will look at three women in the Bible, who were put in harm's way because of what their husbands chose to do. Sometimes as women we can already see the very possible end of something our husbands are intent on doing, or we just want a lot of details that may not be available about something new they feel inspired to do. That is where trusting God has to kick in as never before.

I believe God has a reason for giving a wife this kind of perception that allows us to read into or discern things in a way our husbands cannot. As we fear God and choose to submit to Him on behalf of our families and choose to be that wise woman who wants to build her house **(Prv. 14:1),** then we are able to do good and not be afraid. We're not overcome with evil, but instead we overcome evil with good.

There is favor God has chosen to be obtained through the wife. "Whoso findeth a wife findeth a good thing, and obtaineth favour of the Lord" **(Prov. 18:22).**

The husband may want to disregard this if he's been puffed up with his own pride, by peer pressure from the work place or the locker room, or maybe just from not knowing the word of God.

We will see in the following examples that a holy fear of God and walking with a quiet spirit and behavior that's under control because we

22

In Harm's Way

trust the Lord will bring about great results where danger is eminent.

Jael– wife of Heber the Kenite *(Jael of the Tribe of Judah, her name is Hebrew and means = a wild goat or mountain goat)*

Jdg. 4:4-22

4 And Deborah, a prophetess, the wife of Lapidoth, she judged Israel at that time.

5 And she dwelt under the palm tree of Deborah between Ramah and Bethel in mount Ephraim: and the children of Israel came up to her for judgment.

6 And she sent and called Barak the son of Abinoam out of Kedesh-naphtali, and said unto him, Hath not the Lord God of Israel commanded, saying, Go and draw toward mount Tabor, and take with thee ten thousand men of the children of Naphtali and of the children of Zebulun?

7 And I will draw unto thee to the river Kishon Sisera, the captain of Jabin's army, with his chariots and his multitude; and I will deliver him into thine hand.

8 And Barak said unto her, If thou wilt go with me, then I will go: but if thou wilt not go with me, then I will not go.

9 And she said, I will surely go with thee: notwithstanding the journey that thou takest shall not be for thine honour; for the Lord shall sell Sisera into the hand of a woman: and Deborah arose, and went with Barak to Kedesh.

10 And Barak called Zebulun and Naphtali to Kedesh; and he went up with ten thousand men at his feet: and Deborah went up with him.

Michele Smith

11 Now Heber the Kenite, which was of the children of Hobab the father in law of Moses, had severed himself from the Kenites, and pitched his tent unto the plain of Zaanaim, which is by Kedesh.

12 And they shewed Sisera that Barak the son of Abinoam was gone up to mount Tabor.

13 And Sisera gathered together all his chariots, even nine hundred chariots of iron, and all the people that were with him, from Harosheth of the Gentiles unto the river of Kishon.

14 And Deborah said unto Barak, Up; for this is the day in which the Lord hath delivered Sisera into thine hand: is not the Lord gone out before thee? So Barak went down from mount Tabor, and ten thousand men after him.

15 And the Lord discomfited Sisera, and all his chariots, and all his host, with the edge of the sword before Barak; so that Sisera lighted down off his chariot, and fled way on his feet.

16 But Barak pursued after the chariots, and after the host, unto Harosheth of the Gentiles: and all the host of Sisera fell upon the edge of the sword; and there was not a man left.

17 Howbeit Sisera fled away on his feet to the tent of Jael the wife of Heber the Kenite: for there was peace between Jabin the king of Hazor and the house of Heber the Kenite.

18 And Jael went out to meet Sisera, and said unto him, Turn in, my lord, turn in to me; fear not. And when he had turned in unto her into the tent, she covered him with a mantle.

19 And he said unto her, Give me, I pray thee, a little water to drink; for I am thirsty. And she opened a bottle of milk, and gave him drink, and covered him.

In Harm's Way

20 Again he said unto her, Stand in the door of the tent, and it shall be, when any man doth come and enquire of thee, and say, Is there any man here? that thou shalt say, No.

21 Then Jael Heber's wife took a nail of the tent, and took a hammer in her hand, and went softly unto him, and smote the nail into his temples, and fastened it into the ground: for he was fast asleep and weary. So he died.

22 And, behold, as Barak pursued Sisera, Jael came out to meet him, and said unto him, come, and I will shew thee the man whom thou seekest. And when he came into her tent, behold, Sisera lay dead, and the nail was in his temples.

Let's pause a moment to visualize and get the backdrop of events here.

God has called Deborah a prophetess, the wife of Lapidoth to judge Israel at this time **(Jdg. 4:4).** God also called Barak to go out against Sisera, the commander of Jabin's army, with his chariots and his multitude... to rout this enemy of God's people causing them to cry out to Him.

Deborah, the prophetess, sends for Barak, who just seems reluctant apparently to do what God has told him, who then insist when confronted that unless she goes to the battle, he won't. So she agrees to go but lets him know that he will not get any glory out of this victory because God will give Sisera into the hand of a woman.

Now, Jael whose husband is somewhat friendly with the enemy has his tent pitched near the terebinth tree at Zaanaim, which is beside Kedesh. He's neutral and impartial to the enemy, but something's different with his wife, and we'll see God use her.

Now, can any of us relate to a friendship your husband has had in the past or maybe now, where you as his wife sense something's not right, but you're not able to say anything to him about it? This is what we are looking at here with Jael. It's apparent in the context of scripture that she knew something or better yet, someone and could sense that this was not a God connection. She laid low about it and remained a watchman on the wall.

The Bible doesn't show us in the context of this story that she freaked out or panicked at her husband's poor choice of friends. Jael was a woman in touch with God and her trust was in Him. She possessed a meek and quiet spirit that allowed God to choose her and use her to carry out His purpose in spite of her husband's dealings. Now, that's how I want God to use m e.

We can gather here that Sisera, being exhausted from the battle and fleeing on foot, assumed he had found a place he would be safe since Jael's husband, Heber, was a leader in the tribe of Judah, because they had an alliance with Jabin king of Hazor, but not so.

"So God subdued on that day Jabin the king of Canaan before the children of Israel. And the hand of the children of Israel prospered, and prevailed against Jabin the king of Canaan, until they had destroyed Jabin king of Canaan" **(Jdg. 4:23-24).**

So we see here Jael, a worshipper of God, which caused her to arise courageously to the occasion, in the heat of a dangerous yet significant battle to be used of God for a mighty victory.

Abigail – wife of Nabal, descendent of Caleb (*Abigail is Hebrew and means = "father rejoices."*

1 Sam. 25:2-42

2 And there was a man in Maon, whose possessions were in Carmel; and the man was very great, and he had three thousand sheep, and a thousand goats: and he was shearing his sheep in Carmel.

3 Now the name of the man was Nabal; and the name of his wife Abigail: and she was a woman of good understanding, and of a beautiful countenance: but the man was churlish and evil in his doings; and he was of the house of Caleb.

In Harm's Way

4 And David heard in the wilderness that Nabal did shear his sheep.

5 And David sent out ten young men, and David said unto the young men, Get you up to Carmel, and go to Nabal, and greet him in my name:

6 And thus shall ye say to him that liveth in prosperity, Peace be both to thee, and peace be to thine house, and peace be unto all that thou hast.

7 And now I have heard that thou hast shearers: now thy shepherds which were with us, we hurt them not, neither was there ought missing unto them, all the while they were in Carmel.

8 Ask thy young men, and they will shew thee. Wherefore let the young men find favour in thine eyes: for we come in a good day: give, I pray thee, whatsoever cometh to thine hand unto thy servants, and to thy son David.

9 And when David's young men came, they spake to Nabal according to all those words in the name of David, and ceased.

10 And Nabal answered David's servants, and said, Who is David? and who is the son of Jesse? There be many servants now a days that break away every man from his master.

11 Shall I then take my bread, and my water, and my flesh that I have killed for my shearers, and give it unto men, whom I know not whence they be?

12 So David's young men turned their way, and went again, and came and told him all those sayings.

Michele Smith

13 And David said unto his men, Gird ye on every man his sword. And they girded on every man his sword; and David also girded on his sword: and there went up after David about four hundred men; and two hundred abode by the stuff.

14 But one of the young men told Abigail, Nabal's wife, saying, Behold, David sent messengers out of the wilderness to salute our master; and he railed on them.

15 But the men were very good unto us, and we were not hurt, neither missed we anything, as long as we were conversant with them, when we were in the fields

16 They were a wall unto us both by night and day, all the while we were with them keeping the sheep.

17 Now therefore know and consider what thou wilt do; for evil is determined against our master, and against all his household: for he is such a son of Belial, that a man cannot speak to him.

18 Then Abigail made haste, and took two hundred loaves, and two bottles of wine, and five sheep ready dressed, and five measures of parched corn, and a hundred clusters of raisins, and two hundred cakes of figs, and laid them on asses.

19 And she said unto her servants, Go on before me; behold, I come after you. But she told not her husband Nabal.

20 And it was so, as she rode on the ass, that she came down by the covert on the hill, and, behold, David and his men came down against her; and she met them.

21 Now David had said, surely in vain have I kept all that this fellow hath in the wilderness, so that nothing was missed of all that

In Harm's Way

pertained unto him: and he hath requited me evil for good.

22 So and more also do God unto the enemies of David, if I leave of all that pertain to him by the morning light any that pisseth against the wall.

23 And when Abigail saw David, she hasted, and lighted off the ass, and fell before David on her face, and bowed herself to the ground,

24 And fell at his feet, and said, Upon me, my lord, upon me let this iniquity be: and let thine handmaid, I pray thee, speak in thine audience, and hear the words of thine handmaid.

25 Let not my lord, I pray thee, regard this man of Belial, even Nabal: for as his name is, so is he; Nabal is his name, and folly is with him: but I thine handmaid saw not the young men of my lord, whom thou didst send.

26 Now therefore, my lord, as the Lord liveth, and as thy soul liveth, seeing the Lord hath withholden thee from coming to shed blood, and from avenging thyself with thine own hand, now let thine enemies, and they that seek evil to my lord, be as Nabal.

27 And now this blessing which thine handmaid hath brought unto my lord, let it even be given unto the young men that follow my lord.

28 I pray thee, forgive the trespass of thine handmaid: for the Lord will certainly make my lord a sure house; all thy days.

29 Yet a man is risen to pursue thee, and to seek thy soul: but the soul of my lord shall be bound in the bundle of life with the Lord thy God; and the souls of thine enemies, them shall he sling out, as out of the middle of a sling.

30 And it shall come to pass, when the Lord shall have done to my lord according to all the good that he hath spoken concerning thee, and shall have appointed thee ruler over Israel;

31 That this shall be no grief unto thee, nor offence of heart unto my lord, either that thou hast shed blood causeless, or that my lord hath avenged himself: but when the Lord shall have dealt well with my lord, then remember thine handmaid.

32 And David said to Abigail, Blessed be the Lord God of Israel, which sent thee this day to meet me:

33 And blessed be thy advice, and blessed be thou, which hast kept me this day from coming to shed blood, and from avenging myself with mine own hand.

34 For in very deed, as the Lord God of Israel liveth, which hath kept me back from hurting thee, except thou hadst hasted and come to meet me, surely there had not been left unto Nabal by the morning light any that pisseth against the wall.

35 So David received of her hand that which she had brought him, and said unto her, Go up in peace to thine house; see, I have hearkened to thy voice, and have accepted thy person.

36 And Abigail came to Nabal; and, behold, he held a feast in his house, like the feast of a king; and Nabal's heart was merry within him, for he was very drunken: wherefore she told him nothing, less or more, until the morning light.

37 But it came to pass in the morning, when the wine was gone out of Nabal, and his wife had told him these things, that his heart died within him, and he became as a stone.

In Harm's Way

38 And it came to pass about ten days after, that the Lord smote Nabal, that he died.

39 And when David heard that Nabal was dead, he said, Blessed be the Lord, that hath pleaded the cause of my reproach from the hand of Nabal, and hath kept his servant from evil: for the Lord hath returned the wickedness of Nabal upon his own head. And David sent and communed with Abigail, to take her to him to wife.

40 And when the servants of David were come to Abigail to Carmel, they spake unto her, saying, David sent us unto thee, to take thee to him to wife.

41 And she arose, and bowed herself on her face to the earth, and said, Behold, let thine handmaid be a servant to wash the feet of the servants of my lord.

42 And Abigail hasted, and arose and rode upon an ass, with five damsels of hers that went after her; and she went after the messengers of David, and became his wife.

Here we have David, a man after God's own heart whose has been anointed to be the next king of Israel. He is victorious in Israel and known by all, **(I Sam. 18:6-7)**, fighting God's battles but is on the run because of Saul's jealousy of him. Seeing his men are exhausted and needing care, he sends his servants very respectfully to Nabal to request food at a very festive time. Nabal rails on his servants with his harsh reply, nothing like that of his descendent Caleb.

They return to report to David the reply and he is furious and sets out to annihilate the entire household of Nabal. Thank God Nabal has a wife who is in touch with God, where again we see how she responds to the news of calamity that threatens their whole household because of her husband's harshness.

She goes out to intercede for her family. She not only does that,

31

but she keeps David, God's anointed king from carrying out bloodshed, a later grief of heart in avenging himself **(Verses 36-37).**

Here again we see Abigail, a wise, beautiful woman with a good understanding, as the scripture refers to her in Verse 3, was available to stand in the gap and divert danger caused by the foolish behavior of her husband. This definitely was one of the worst-case scenarios of a crisis marriage relationship. She honors the king, also respecting her husband and was very wise knowing when to talk to him and when to wait.

She ends up being David's wife.

David remembered her and God remembers us too. We are His bride, the bride of Christ.

Sarah – wife of Abraham *(Sarah is Hebrew and means = "prin-cess")*

We find another example of circumstances that can provoke wives to fear because of our husbands' actions, intentional or unintentional.

Gen. 12:10-15:

10 And there was a famine in the land: and Abram went down into Egypt to sojourn there; for the famine was grievous in the land.

11 And it came to pass, when he was come near to enter into Egypt, that he said unto Sarai his wife, Behold now, I know that thou art a fair woman to look upon:

12 Therefore it shall come to pass, when the Egyptians shall see thee, that they shall say, this is his wife: and they will kill me, but they will save thee alive.

13 Say, I pray thee, thou art my sister: that it may be well with me for thy sake; and my soul shall live because of thee.

14 And it came to pass, that, when Abram was come into Egypt, the Egyptians beheld the woman that she was very fair.

15 The princes also of Pharaoh saw her, and commended her before Pharaoh: and the woman was taken into Pharaoh's house.

Let's look at the possible danger in this situation. She could have been raped, taken as another man's wife. Defilement would mean that

In Harm's Way

another man had taken her or slept with her. It may have been in question whether she even could be taken back as Abraham's wife.

That's scary, I don't think when it says in **1 Peter 3:6** to do good and not be afraid that it means we won't face fear or become startled, but will we become paralyzed or immobilized?

Here is where our reaction would indicate whether our trust is grounded in the Lord or not. Do we run to God in prayer with unwavering trust and listen for instruction, or do we become frozen with fear, unable to do anything at all. That is why encouragement from witnesses **(Heb. 12:1)** and the testimony of others is so powerful.

As believers, we all face fears often. Ask Joshua, Gideon, Paul, Abigail, Sarah, your coworker, a friend or the sister sitting in the pew next to you. The things that come to shake us will determine whether we go forward in faith or fold in these very real times of challenges. We are subject to all kinds of fears: fear for our life, our marriage, our children, world crisis, and many other things; but it is God Who makes all the difference. He is "I AM" **(Ex. 3:14; Jn. 10:10)**, Jesus Christ is the answer to all we will ever face. He is very present to help.

God tells us in **Isaiah 51:2**, to look also to Sarah who bore us; this refers to being believers in Jesus Christ. As women, we are specifically designed to multi-task. Most of what we do are behind the scenes and often goes unnoticed. We set the tone in our homes and community.

We are often in great demand to assist our husbands, children, grandchildren and others. For those of us who have sold out and are devoted to true worship **(Jn. 4:23)**, having the love of our husbands, their support, encouragement and covering are so important, but what happens if that love and covering is not there or expressed when you need it? What then? As believers, we are specially marked as a target for opposition from the world and the devil because we are a vital key God uses against the works of darkness to show forth His glory.

I've learned through studying Sarah that she really had something powerful going on with the Lord, as well as with Abraham. She was sensitive to the concerns of her husband, respectful.

Trusting the Lord, she had that meek and quiet spirit **(1 Peter 3:6).** Nowhere in this context of scripture does it show that she snapped or panicked. It doesn't show any response from her, but it does show a response from God because of her faith and submission.

I can recall being led to respecting my husband as my head, and so yielding, out of obedience to the call of God, I did quietly with continuous At times, people looked at me like, "Is she crazy?" The result was the saving power of God at work for my family, from glory to glory. God is continually at work in us performing and helping us to grow and mature in Him.

"Being confident of this very thing, that he which hath begun a good work in you will perform it until the day of Jesus Christ"**(Phil. 1:6).**

I'm sure you can recall some things too, and you should praise Him. He's been there for us more than we know. Some may say well in that culture the women were of little value, equated to that of an animal, and that may have been so in that culture, but look at the response of God in Sarah's behalf.

"And the Lord plagued Pharaoh and his house with great plagues because of Sarai Abram's wife" **(Gen. 12:17).**

Oh, the display of His glory **(Eph. 1:12)!** That is always what God wants to achieve in and through us. I love where evidence can be seen that God was and is at work, where I can see His fingerprints all over the place even in the small things working in my family and in me. It helps me to be poised differently for the next crisis that comes. God is faithfully working in our lives, just as He was working in the lives of Abraham and Sarah, unfolding His awesome plan for their lives. They both made mistakes but grew to be the people from which we find encouragement.

Ladies, when people don't genuinely validate you and even those closest to you fail to appreciate and value you, know that God does. Stay humble and understand that He sees you, and sees you as very precious, having a value that far exceeds rubies, and He will cause your honor to be known by all in due time.

"Humble yourselves therefore under the mighty hand of God, that he may exalt you in due time" **(1 Pet. 5:6).**

This is exclusively spoken of the "virtuous woman," who according to

In Harm's Way

Proverbs 31:10 is a rare find. Get this and hear the word, you will not often find such like her because she's submitted to God and her husband. She's in the marketplace but you can find good evidence of her being home. Look out, as you research this topic, unfortunately you will quickly find how distasteful and controversial the topic of submission is. Be prepared because you will encounter people who want to make the truth of God of no effect, explaining away His goodness and trying to deflate your joy and stop you from the important work of building your house, being a homemaker as the world calls it.

Sanballat and Tobiah **(Neh. 4)** did this when Nehemiah was helping Israel build the walls that had been all broken down and burned up. Nehemiah remained faithful on the wall not allowing the distractions and diversions of the enemy to prevail, but stayed with the work and kept the sword (the Word of God)**(Eph. 6:17)** strapped to his side **(Neh. 4:18)**, so should we. I believe one of the results and greater works of God would be fewer failed marriages as we trust and give the Lord opportunity to show up and show off for us more and more **(Prv. 14:1, 31:27)**.

Psalm 91 is a powerful promise of God's presence, protection and help. I would like to encourage women professing godliness with it for it gives great comfort and reassurance when we find ourselves in harm's way. This is a mentoring time where David was encouraging Solomon in this Psalm, and so I encourage you and me with it. My mom personally gave me this passage when I first moved out on my own at 24. Be encouraged, beloved sister. You are doing a good work *that is not going unnoticed, remember that.*

Psalm 91

1 He that dwelleth in the secret place of the most High shall abide under the shadow of the Almighty.

2 I will say of the Lord, He is my refuge and my fortress: my God; in him will I trust.

Michele Smith

3 Surely he shall deliver thee from the snare of the fowler, and from the noisome pestilence.

4 He shall cover thee with his feathers, and under his wings shalt thou trust: his truth shall be thy shield and buckler.

5 Thou shalt not be afraid for the terror by night; nor for the arrow that flieth by day;

6 Nor for the pestilence that walketh in darkness; nor for the destruction that wasteth at noonday.

7 A thousand shall fall at thy side, and ten thousand at thy right hand; but it shall not come nigh thee.

8 Only with thine eyes shalt thou behold and see the reward of the wicked.

9 Because thou hast made the Lord, which is my refuge, even the most High, thy habitation;

10 There shall no evil befall thee, neither shall any plague come nigh thy dwelling.

11 For he shall give his angels charge over thee, to keep thee in all thy ways.

12 They shall bear thee up in their hands, lest thou dash thy foot against a stone.

13 Thou shalt tread upon the lion and adder: the young lion and the dragon shalt thou trample under feet.

In Harm's Way

14 Because he hath set his love upon me, therefore will I deliver him: I will set him on high, because he hath known my name.

15 He shall call upon me, and I will answer him: I will be with him in trouble; I will deliver him, and honour him.

16 With long life will I satisfy him, and shew him my salvation.

Thanks, Mom. I love you
(Blanche M. Fuller 1928-2010-Eternity)

Women in Intercession

Interceding for souls, warring for destinies

Understanding Our Ministry of the Home

Submission to God is very important to the home. The Bible says. In the previous chapter, I talked about how God includes us, womankind, to share with Him in the work of building, kingdom building; building our homes **(Prv. 14:1)** and what an honor this is contributing to the outcome of lives. Many miss this and really do not look at it as a position of honor. The reason is that instead of being valued and appreciated, we often seem to be degraded, dumped on and forgotten.

To gain significance many of us get caught up with competing in the corporate world and the church. We compete with or try to usurp men, at worst maliciously tearing them down and slandering them with our words, feeling justified because of what we experienced. Jesus is standing there watching us go off in our own direction and waiting for us to get on the right path.

"Come unto me, all ye that labour and are heavy laden, and I will give you rest" **(Mt. 11:28)**.

This is not about negating women in ministry, other leadership positions or professional roles in the career paths we take, but I am negating any that have taken on roles through a wrong spirit like rebellion, envy or revenge. Please be careful that you do not go into ministry with a sin-tainted spirit because it is likely to poison and infect everything.

"Looking diligently lest any man fail of the grace of God; lest any root of bitterness springing up trouble you, and thereby many be defiled **(Heb. 12:15)**.

Jesus said when Peter got the revelation of Him, "And I say also unto thee, That thou art Peter, and upon this rock I will build my church; and the gates of hell shall not prevail against it" **(Mt. 16:18)**.

One morning, the Lord woke me up with these words so loud in my spirit that it literally caused me to sit up: *"I am building my church!"*

38

Women in Intercession

I felt he was encouraging my faith and confidence in Him as I had been warring so for souls in my family and the warfare had been so long and intense. God is faithful to encourage us as we are pursuing His purpose and following His path for our lives. I felt He was directly telling me,"Don't be weary, don't be discouraged, and don't you forget, this is *my* work you are committed to and *I am* doing it!"

All believers are a part of His kingdom-building work, some in different ways than others. Again, I emphasize that we all take part. We are partakers, members of the body of Christ *(the church)*, and we need each other functioning properly in our God-designed roles *(in the natural)* in this world.

My focus in this book, as I felt led to write, is highlighting the role of womankind, particularly wives **(Mt. 16:18, Prov. 14:1).** We share in the Lord's building work, but not with brick and mortar as in construction or masonry. This is more about the work of building relationships *(*reconciling)*, lives and homes that have the potential to impact neighborhoods, communities and nations. Building as women is done largely through our God-given design and ability to nurture, to help *(by the Spirit)* and influence, fueling all that we do by prayer.

"And all things are of God, who hath reconciled us to himself by Jesus Christ, and hath given to us the ministry of reconciliation"**(2 Cor. 5:18).**

"And ye shall teach them your children, speaking of them when thou sittest in thine house, and when thou walkest by the way, when thou liest down, and when thou risest up" **Deut. 11:19).**

We watch over our homes. We are the help meet of our husbands and their companions, offering support and encouragement to them, our family and others. We cultivate an environment of peace in our homes that trick- les into our neighborhoods and communities. This is so powerful by the love and life of Jesus Christ that we allow to flow through us so readily by the Holy Spirit. As believers, we maintain a worshipful spirit and develop through trusting God that meek and quiet spirit mentioned in **1 Peter 3:4.**

We recognize the gifts and talents of our children early on and ponder: *keeping in mind* **(Luke 2:51)** as Mary did after observing her child's gifts, speaking into the lives of many, words of life, giving them meaning.

We pray they will hold on to our words and that they would be constant reminders of divine purpose in a world moving fast, ready to take any off course into derailment and destruction.

There is a destiny thief and an unrelenting robber of souls. When we do not have this building work operating *(the obscure behind-the-scenes seed planting, fertilizing work)* properly through women, we have the startling reality that many die, never fulfilling their God given role and purpose. A life without meaning is like a wreck waiting to happen, but God--**(Jn. 10:10).**

"Where there is no vision, the people perish..." **(Prv. 29:18).**
True purpose *(Gods original intent)* begins with the knowledge of Jesus Christ, who through revelation *(like Peter)* brings us into divine purpose, and to miss the significance of this distinct work in our lives, can leave us robbed of life's purpose and joy that comes from a fulfilled life.

"My people are destroyed for lack of knowledge: because thou hast rejected knowledge, I will also reject thee, that thou shalt be no priest to me: seeing thou hast forgotten the law of thy God, I will also forget thy children" **(Hos. 4:6).**

Homemaking, as the world calls it, often is looked upon as unemployment. The devil is a liar! In fact, just the opposite is true. When we are too preoccupied with vying for status and promotion in the corporate world, church auxiliaries and community affairs, we must be careful not to find that in the eyes of our Maker we are actually MIA *(missing in action)* and insubordinate to the home. When this happens, we will have children longing for priceless and vital validation. If we fail to give it, the god of this world *(the devil),* the thief, is eager to put in his two bits with his destructive ripple effect.

Women in Intercession

"Neither give place to the devil" (Eph. 4:27). Desolation is the result, and lost people, the house torn down and in ruins by our own efforts or lack thereof.

The Bible says the virtuous woman is a crown to her husband. Please don't misunderstand me, this God-given role and work of women in the home does not mean in any way that she has nothing else going on. To the contrary, she's powerful. We as women are able to multi-task

(Prov. 31:10-31).

10 Who can find a virtuous woman? for her price is far above rubies

11 The heart of her husband doth safely trust in her, so that he shall have no need of spoil.

12 She will do him good and not evil all the days of her life.

13 She seeketh wool, and flax, and worketh willingly with her hands 14 She is like the merchants' ships; she bringeth her food from afar.

15 She riseth also while it is yet night, and giveth meat to her household, and a portion to her maidens.

16 She considereth a field, and buyeth it: with the fruit of her hands she planteth a vineyard.

17 She girdeth her loins with strength, and strengtheneth her arms. 18 She perceiveth that her merchandise is good: her candle goeth not out by night.

19 She layeth her hands to the spindle, and her hands hold the distaff.

20 She stretcheth out her hand to the poor; yea, she reacheth forth her hands to the needy.

21 She is not afraid of the snow for her household: for all her household are clothed with scarlet.

22 She maketh herself coverings of tapestry; her clothing is silk and purple.

23 Her husband is known in the gates, when he sitteth among the elders of the land.

24 She maketh fine linen, and selleth it; and delivereth girdles unto the merchant.

25 Strength and honour are her clothing; and she shall rejoice in time to come.

26 She openeth her mouth with wisdom; and in her tongue is the law of kindness.

27 She looketh well to the ways of her household, and eateth not the bread of idleness.

28 Her children arise up, and call her blessed; her husband also, and he praiseth her.

29 Many daughters have done virtuously, but thou excellest them all.

30 Favour is deceitful, and beauty is vain: but a woman that feareth the Lord, she shall be praised.

31 Give her of the fruit of her hands; and let her own works praise her in the gates.

She is an attentive loving wife, mother and individual. She's productive, dependable. and a business woman, a caring person, giver, hard worker and so on.

Women in Intercession

Submission a Controversial Subject

Notice that **Prv. 31:10** is a question, *"Who can find...?"* Why? Because she is a rare find, this is not everyone. She's a woman who has acquired wisdom and an understanding of submission and exemplified it; something which in our world today is despised.

Submission is a very controversial and a touchy subject, even among believers. You may be cringing right now, and it's OK, we always have the Spirit to guide us into all truth.

"But the anointing which ye have received of him abideth in you, and ye need not that any man teach you: but as the same anointing teacheth you of all things, and is truth, and is no lie, and even as it hath taught you, ye shall abide in him" **(1 Jn. 2:27)**.

That is also why I feel so at ease sharing, because we have the Holy Spirit. Just take what's for you and leave what is not. Test this for yourself. Bring up submission when you go to work or to your next women's gathering or ladies' night out, and you'll see the reactions.

When we lack understanding of submission and protocol, some of the challenges and issues to consider is women moving forward too eagerly in ministry positions, taking on leadership roles and less of our men rising to the occasion.

We see women taking charge prematurely and men who will let them and readily relinquish their own responsibility and leadership that's so needed, just as Adam did in the garden *(Gen. 3:6)*.

The other side of this, and we certainly have to commend many women and give God thanks for them because what if no one takes up the ball? I've had the privilege of speaking with some pastors who know God has called women to ministry and leadership but who are careful in implementing it because of the concern that fewer men will take leadership responsibility.

We have to pray for *balance*, timing and the Spirit's continual leading. Again, reactions to the subject of submission from most will surprise, if not shock you. My own initial reaction shocked me when, being led to submit in ways I had not been used to as a wife, God began working this principle in my life, unlocking the mystery of it. It was actually an answer to my prayer

43

to be a virtuous, godly wife, which I truly desired, but again I was surprised to realize where I really stood on the topic.

Warfare

When we begin putting our hand to the plow in kingdom building *warfare* also begins. In calling me to ministry, the Lord first led me to get my priorities in order. Later, after seeing some particular needs in my family, I got a call from a friend who gave me these scripture passages:

"See, I have this day set thee over the nations and over the kingdoms, to root out, and to pull down, and to destroy, and to throw down, to build, and to plant" **(Jer. 1:10)**.

"And they shall fight against thee; but they shall not prevail against thee; for I am with thee, saith the Lord, to deliver thee"**(Jer. 1:19)**.

"Except the Lord build the house, they labour in vain that build it: except the Lord keep the city, the watchman waketh but in vain..... As arrows are in the hand of a mighty man; so are children of the youth. Happy is the man that hath his quiver full of them: they shall not be ashamed, but they shall speak with the enemies in the gate" **(Ps. 127:1, 4-5)**.

The warfare in which we engage is not physical but spiritual **(Eph. 6:12-13)**, and comes as a result of many things: The biggest one is salvation through Jesus Christ, our coming into the kingdom of God as *born-again believers*, children of God; also because of *our purpose and calling*.

For marriage, the attack is fierce and it comes finding access through the *baggage* that we may bring, emotional, financial and spiritual, the generational baggage of our ancestors, all of which we have to shed when God calls us. Certainly, warfare comes largely through our enemy, *the devil*, who hates God and hates marriage and will take advantage of all our areas of weakness. This list is not all-inclusive.

"This charge I commit unto thee, son Timothy, according to the prophecies which went before on thee, that thou by them mightest war a good warfare" **(1 Tim. 1:18)**;

"No man that warreth entangleth himself with the affairs of this life; that he may please him who hath chosen him to be a soldier"**(2 Tim. 2:4)**.

Women in Intercession

Our final and unending quest once we are saved is learning to love God *(grow, develop and cultivate)* and have this love evident in our words, actions and our attitude. God's love is so powerful, when regeneration happens in us, there starts a journey of coming out of agreement with the world's way *(stinkin' thinkin')*, the flesh and the devil and coming into alignment with God and His way. We learn to love what He loves and hate what He hates, being transformed by God's word.

"And be not conformed to this world: but be ye transformed by the renewing of your mind, that ye may prove what is that good, and acceptable, and perfect, will of God"**(Rom. 12:2).**

We can't passively sit back and let the devil tear things up around us; we fight him with the blood of the Jesus, with the Word of God, with our love for our Lord and for each other. Loving God is synonymous with obeying Him, and through that, we wreck the devil's plans, abort his schemes as we determine to be led by the Lord. Hate certainly has its proper place:

"For the Lord, the God of Israel, saith that he hateth putting away: for one covereth violence with his garment, saith the Lord of hosts: therefore take heed to your spirit, that ye deal not treacherously" **(Mal. 2:16).**

"These six things doth the Lord hate: yea, seven are an abomination unto him: A proud look, a lying tongue, and hands that shed innocent blood"**(Prv. 6:16-17).**

"Do not I hate them, O Lord, that hate thee? and am not I grieved with those that rise up against thee? I hate them with perfect hatred: I count them mine enemies" **(Ps. 139:21-22).**

"The fear of the Lord is to hate evil: pride, and arrogancy, and the evil way, and the froward mouth, do I hate" **(Prv. 8:13).**

We learn God's love, but need to know what He hates.
"So then because thou art lukewarm, and neither cold nor hot, I will spew thee out of my mouth" **(Rev. 3:16).**

Now, examine yourself here and if you find that you are neutral or lukewarm, in cahoots with the devil or just unsure, you can pray as David prayed.

Michele Smith

"Search me, O God, and know my heart: try me, and know my thoughts: And see if there be any wicked way in me, and lead me in the way everlasting" **(Ps. 139:23-24).**

This is not an easy prayer, but one I have purposed to become a daily prayer in my life because I know that in my flesh (my carnal earthly nature) that there is never any good thing **(Rom. 7:18).**

Through difficult experiences in my life, the Lord has taught me that daily I have to bring my flesh under and into subjection to the Spirit of Christ.

I pray this prayer because I can't trust in my own self-examination alone. I need God's too. His word says, "The heart is deceitful above all things, and desperately wicked: who can know it" **(Jer. 17:9)?** Before this, it says in **(Jer. 17:5),** "Thus saith the Lord; Cursed be the man that trusteth in man, and maketh flesh his arm, and whose heart departeth from the Lord."

Thank God that as I am consistent in praying this way, I find that it's not as hard for the Lord to take me from glory to glory. Sometimes it does take me awhile, but I am ever striving to get there.

Sacrifice of Being an Effective Warrior

There is a price for her *(the virtuous woman)*, **(Prv. 31:12-27).** The cost is in appropriating the word, applying it, coming out of agreement with anything not of God **(Jn. 14:30),** taking the straight and narrow way, spending time in His Presence.

"Hereafter I will not talk much with you: for the prince of this world cometh, and hath nothing in me" **(Jn. 14:30)**

This is the longing desire of every serious believer and the wrestling of Jacob, because while in this world, in these present bodies, we still have to deal with both old and new nature, which are constantly at war with one another, putting one down and taking up the other **(Gal. 5:17; Eph. 4:21-24).**

Women in Intercession

Therein the first level of warfare is getting out of our flesh and purposefully moving by way of the Spirit of God. *Get yourself free first!*

The Bible says:"Awake, awake; put on thy strength, O Zion [another name for the church]; put on thy beautiful garments, O Jerusalem, the holy city: for henceforth there shall no more come into thee the uncircumcised and the unclean. Shake thyself from the dust; arise, and sit down, O Jerusalem: loose thyself from the bands of thy neck, O captive daughter of Zion"**(Is. 52:1-2).**

"How long wilt thou go about, O backsliding daughter.."**(Jer. 31:22)?**

The reference to daughters points again and again to Sarah who bore you *(paraphrased)* **(Is. 51:2).** This is a call not to the unbeliever but to the believer, the Church *(the bigger picture)*, and marriage is our earthly por-trait, the wife is our subject. Greater works await women of God!

Testimony

As a young girl in grade school, almost every year I would write about the same person for my biography report in history — Harriet Tubman. I was captivated by her. She was a married woman who could not let go of a burning desire within to be free from slavery. What began with first her freedom resulted in the freedom of many others. History records the many times she went back to get others free in spite of an injury she sustained in slavery that caused her to have random blackouts and the danger of having a bounty on her head. She was never once caught because she and the Underground Railroad abolitionists, whom she joined and worked along with, were all a work of God.

Later, in my adult life, I realized it was my desire to help others get to freedom when God delivered me, freeing me to operate in the divine purpose of God for my life in the kingdom work and kingdom building. It has been also confirmed repeatedly that God has called me definitely to mission work.

Michele Smith

Intercession and Warfare

- **Shiprah And Puah**

We'll look here at some women in scripture regarding intercession for souls. These women are found in **Ex. 1** as Hebrew midwives who feared God.

"And the king of Egypt spake to the Hebrew midwives, of which the name of the one was Shiphrah, and the name of the other Puah: And he said, When ye do the office of a midwife to the Hebrew women, and see them upon the stools; if it be a son, then ye shall kill him: but if it be a daughter, then she shall live. But the midwives feared God, and did not as the king of Egypt commanded them, but saved the men children alive" **(Ex. 1:15-17).**

Imagine this scene: the midwives were present and aiding the Hebrew women as they gave birth. The Bible mentions only these two, but there were probably other midwives. **Shiprah** *(beauty)*, and **Puah** *(blast)*, assisted in the birth of girls and boys but disobeyed the order to kill the male babies and were later called in by the Pharaoh, who asked, "Why have ye done this thing, and have saved the men children alive" **(Ex. 1:18)?**

Can you see the dilemma of these two women who refused to be used by the devil? Risking their own lives, they could have been killed, *but God!* Because of their courage and faith, God blessed them with families of their own.

"And the midwives said unto Pharaoh, Because the Hebrew women are not as the Egyptian women; for they are lively, and are delivered ere the midwives come in unto them. Therefore God dealt well with the midwives: and the people multiplied, and waxed very mighty. And it came to pass, be-cause the midwives feared God, that he made them houses" **(Ex. 1:19-21).**

Wow! What an example of service and encouragement for women who are single and desiring to be married, a season we all have. Here is a clear example of us needing each other and interacting together, single and married women. Yes, there is a need for individual ministry to both groups *(single/married)*, but there is also a need to interact with one another.

Women in Intercession

We are missing something if we are only involved with people who are like us. There is no need for competition and jealousy. They are tools of the devil, who is happy to use them to divide us. For the virgin or unmarried *(single)* woman is void of the conflict we have as married women and has the blessed privilege of being able to devote herself freely and wholly to the Lord. We all need each other!

"There is a difference also between a wife and a virgin. The unmarried woman careth for the things of the Lord, that she may be holy both in body and in spirit: but she that is married careth for the things of the world, how she may please her husband. And this I speak for your own profit; not that I may cast a snare upon you, but for that which is comely, and that ye may attend upon the Lord without distraction"**(1 Cor. 7:34-35).**

• Jehoshabeath

Another example in scripture dealing with intercession and warfare is in **2 Chronicles 22**, regarding a woman name Jehoshabeath:

"But when Athaliah the mother of Ahaziah saw that her son was dead, she arose and destroyed all the seed royal of the house of Judah. But Jehoshabeath, the daughter of the king, took Joash the son of Ahaziah, and stole him from among the king's sons that were slain, and put him and his nurse in a bedchamber. So Jehoshabeath, the daughter of king Jehoram, the wife of Jehoiada the priest, (for she was the sister of Ahaziah,) hid him from Athaliah, so that she slew him not. And he was with them hid in the house of God six years: and Athaliah reigned over the land**(2 Chr. 22:10-12).**

"And in the seventh year Jehoiada strengthened himself..., And all the congregation made a covenant with the king in the house of God. And he said unto them, Behold, the king's son shall reign, as the Lord hath said of the sons of David"**(2 Chr. 23:1,-3).**

Joash became king at the age of seven and was a good king, which was rare among the many kings appointed, but he would have never been king had not a woman's intercession taken place.

49

His destiny would have been wiped out, but for God working through the courage of this woman, Jehoshabeath.

"Joash was seven years old when he began to reign, and he reigned forty years in Jerusalem. His mother's name also was Zibiah of Beersheba"**(2 Chr. 24:1).**

Notice it was not his mother here who stepped in and saved his life. I am grateful for some of the godly women who have interceded, embraced and encouraged my children. His mother probably was just as grateful.

• Esther

The last example of intercession and warfare we'll review is that of Esther whose courage affected not only her family but also the whole nation of Israel. What I also want you to take note of here is her manner, her submission and her willingness to take risks like the others.

She was in such an advantageous position as the wife of the king and could have played it safe. As the plan of Haman to destroy the Jews, God's people, was brought to her attention **(Esther 4:7-8),** this was her dilemma: Even as queen, Esther could not go into the king's court unless he's summoned her.

"All the king's servants, and the people of the king's provinces, do know, that whosoever, whether man or women, shall come unto the king into the inner court, who is not called, there is one law of his to put him to death, except such to whom the king shall hold out the golden sceptre, that he may live: but I have not been called to come in unto the king these thirty days"**(Es. 4:11).**

So here we find her concerned for her life, but her uncle, who had raised her after her parents died, responds to her with this message:

"...Think not with thyself that thou shalt escape in the king's house, more than all the Jews. For if thou altogether holdest thy peace at this time, then shall there enlargement and deliverance arise to the Jews from another place; but thou and thy father's house shall be destroyed: and who knoweth whether thou art come to the kingdom for such a time as this"**(Es. 4:13-14)?**

Women in Intercession

She responds in courage, resolving to take the risk and go before the king unsummoned, even if it cost her life, but first asking her people to fast with her for three days,

"...and so will I go in unto the king, which is not according to the law: and if I perish, I perish"**(Es. 4:16).**

When the three days of fasting were up,"Esther put on her royal apparel, and stood in the inner court of the king's house"**(Es. 5:1).**

We read on to find that the king extends the golden scepter to her, and with wisdom, she exposes the plan of Haman (who represents the devil) to the king and brings about his demise **(Es. 7:1-10).**

Yet even after that, we find in **Esther 8 and 9** that there is still a need for intercession and a plan of action or strategy because of what the Haman had already set in motion. So here again we examine and study the attitude, the behavior of Queen Esther before the king.

"And Esther spake yet again before the king, and fell down at his feet, and besought him with tears to put away the mischief of Haman the Agagite, and his device that he had devised against the Jews. Then the king held out the golden sceptre toward Esther. So Esther arose, and stood before the king, And said, If it please the king, and if I have favour in his sight, and the thing seem right before the king, and I be pleasing in his eyes, let it be written to reverse the letters devised by Haman the son of Hammedatha the Agagite, which he wrote to destroy the Jews which are in all the king's provinces: For how can I endure to see the evil that shall come unto my people? or how can I endure to see the destruction of my kindred" **(Es. 8:3-6)?**

As we continue through chapters 8 and 9 of Esther, the victory was won as the Jews were given permission to defend themselves against any that wanted to destroy them. Then an annual celebration was established to remember God's goodness and intervention for His people. As Jesus makes us aware in **John 10:10** that the thief comes and what is his agenda? *"to steal, and to kill, and to destroy."* Though he is already a defeated foe, there is action we must take to intercede and to battle as fiercely and even more so as he *(the devil)* does.

We have the advantage and the Higher Authority as Esther did because the Greater One (Jesus Christ) is in us and He is greater than he that is in the world. It is in Jesus and through our faith in Him that we pray and carry out prophetic actions to experience the victory. We should not be naïve about this. Look around and see all the casualties that naivety brings about.

The devil stays on his agenda and even more fiercely because he knows his time is short **(Rev. 12:12)** and so we even more so must come together and more boldly in the Spirit's power lay hold of the victory for which Jesus bled and died for us to have.

Testimony and Prophetic Word Confirmed!

"Now in the twelfth month, that is, the month Adar, on the thirteenth day of the same, [March 7, according to the Hebrew lunar calendar] when the king's commandment and his decree drew near to be put in execution, in the day that the enemies of the Jews hoped to have power over them, (though it was turned to the contrary, that the Jews had rule over them that hated them;" When I happened to be reading this particular scripture, I sensed the illumination of the Spirit of God, clearly letting me know that in the year 2013, it would be necessary to war like never before, but that the victory was sure **(Jn. 10:10)**.

This may not seem as clear to you, but God made it so for me. As I began to journey in the Word of God *(The Holy Bible)* some 24 years ago, I found that anything I was curious and wanted to know about I could go to Him (God, The King of kings) like Esther, I would get my answers.
As I asked, searched, prayed, trusted Him and waited, He would answer.

For instance, on my Mom's side of the family, people believed in a lot of superstitious stuff I was uncomfortable with as a growing believer, and I did not want it to influence my life. One of those superstitions was with the number 13.

Women in Intercession

So years ago, I asked God and searched for references in the Bible to that number. This number was in Es. 3:12; 9:1; 9:17-18 and to my surprise it had evil connotations, evil purposed against God's people in reference to it.

Yet there in the book of Esther was also the turnaround for good to God's people. Esther, through Mordecai, her uncle's encouragement and leadership took a leap of faith and went before the king, thus causing the plan of the enemy to be reverse on his own head.

"And Harbonah, one of the chamberlains, said before the king, Behold also, the gallows fifty cubits high, which Haman had made for Mordecai,who spoken good for the king, standeth in the house of Haman. Then the king said, Hang him thereon"**(Es. 7:9).**

I was and am again encouraged. I hope you are too. It was also confirmed through a man of God flowing in a strong prophetic anointing in my church fellowship, this was the first time he had ever spoken to me, and he told me that it was going to be necessary for me to contend.

"...ye should earnestly contend for the faith which was once delivered unto the saints" **(Jude 1:3).**

He said that he already knew I was a contender or prayer warrior but emphasized that I was going to have to contend as never before. I didn't believe this was just for me, so I shared this each time God had given me an opportunity with others; encouraging them to go in for the victory for themselves, their family, friends, church fellowship, our country and leadership.

Summary

Like it or not, in this world as children of God, we are already enlisted as soldiers and are in a warfare Day 1 and on. Another place in the Bible I found the number 13, **(Gen. 17:25)** the age at which Ishmael, the son born to Abraham through the surrogate plan of Sarah *(through Hagar)*, was circumcised. Again, we see an evil connotation because we know though he was born before Isaac. He was not the promised child.

One other is **1 Kings 7:1,** which says it took Solomon 13 years to build his palace. It's not that I would even give numbers so much attention except since my youngest child *(our surprise baby)* was born in the year 2000, every year after I have sensed the Lord specifically enlightening me of some significance, so I humbly give attention to Him and take heed.

In Conclusion of This Chapter

Esther had the golden scepter extended to her, we as believers also have the Scepter extended to us through Christ's righteousness, which, if we really think about it, should cause us to rejoice exceedingly, as well.

"For he hath made him to be sin for us, who knew no sin; that we might be made the righteousness of God in him"**(2 Cor. 5:21).**

So now we are able to come boldly unto His throne, Hallelujah!

"But unto the Son he saith, Thy throne, O God, is for ever and ever: a sceptre of righteousness is the sceptre of thy kingdom"**(Heb. 1:8).**

"Thy throne, O God, is for ever and ever: the sceptre of thy kingdom is a right scepter" **(Ps. 45:6).**

For every child of God defeats this evil world, and we achieve this victory through our faith. Who can win this battle against the world? *Only those who believe that Jesus is the Son of God.*

Women in Intercession

"For whatsoever is born of God overcometh the world: and this is the victory that overcometh the world, even our faith. Who is he that overcometh the world, but he that believeth that Jesus is the Son of God"**(1 Jn. 5:4-5).**

You Are Going to Have This Baby!

"And being not weak in faith, he considered not his own body now dead, when he was about a hundred years old, neither yet the deadness of Sarah's womb"**(Rom. 4:19).**

Now pulling from the last chapter as we continued on the journey of submission, let me be a **Puah** in your life. ("Puah"= a blast), but please know I have said these very words looking into a mirror. Please pardon me while I encourage myself in the Lord. *(I am literally taking a pause here. I don't want to be a liar, not practicing what I preach).*

Yeah, I said it, the big **P** word, and I am a woman, and believe me, when God called me, I couldn't even say this word. Later, I could say it without crying and going into a prayer of total surrender because more than anything or anyone, I fear going outside the perfect will of God, and secondly, I like my womaness. *(Sorry. I know I'm making up a word.)* I like being prissy.

You are going to have this baby, this vision, this business, this ministry or whatever you know what it is for you! It will not be aborted because it is a work of God, His plan, His word that will not return to Him empty (void).

"So shall my word be that goeth forth out of my mouth: it shall not return unto me void, but it shall accomplish that which I please, and it shall prosper in the thing whereto I sent it"**(Is. 55:11).**

I'm not talking about coveting what is someone else's or just pulling something randomly out of the air. I am hitting hard on that God-ordained thing you know is from Him. If you don't know, I pray you would be spurred on to get in His Presence and in His word to find out. I challenge you to look in the mirror too and begin to say this to yourself. Say it several times until it doesn't feel so awkward, weak or phony, especially if you have had to pick up your esteem and yourself off the floor as I have.

You Are Going to Have This Baby!

You might have felt beat down by the world, circumstances, people you thought loved and believed in you or you have failed to keep up the vital intimacy of your love relationship with Christ and have let your own self down.

Please hear me again, *You are going to have this baby! You will birth the purpose, the plan of God for your life!* Don't lose heart. He loves you! I love you! And we have got to love and encourage each other.

At the end of this chapter, I will challenge you to write in a brief statement. Who are you? Sounds simple, huh? Well, let me add this piece to it. Who are you according to God's plan?

"For I know the thoughts that I think toward you, saith the Lord, thoughts of peace, and not of evil, to give you an expected end" **(Jer. 29:11).**

Genesis 11:30 tells us Sarai was barren. God spoke to me years ago of "Sarah's daughters" with such emphasis in just His steady, clear, still small, consistent voice that I had to pay attention *(Selah).* I began to search the scriptures and seek to understand Him in this, giving attention to get all He has for me out of it and enough to share with others. I knew that He wanted me to be a godly wife and be an example for and to encourage others just as much as I desired to be.

Marriage and family had long been my burden from the time I was just a young girl in grade school. Four years prior to receiving this word, I had come into a church fellowship where they encouraged me to read the Bible, study and embrace the much-needed Helper, the Holy Spirit. This started me on a powerful and glorious journey of faith to understand and appreciate my purpose for being here. This was very fulfilling for me. It brought definition and meaning to my life, and it has given me great joy ever since. I praise God for that!

Although Sarai was beautiful and had a husband who loved her, she had an empty place in her heart where she struggled with her barrenness. Yet she had a promise. She had a word from God. She experienced great despair and anguish **(Is. 54)** thinking that she would never bear a child.

Hannah also, in **1 Samuel** was dearly loved by her husband, but like Sarai experienced barrenness, anguish and misunderstanding.

Her husband couldn't understand her unhappiness and anguish **(1 Sam. 1:8),** and even Eli, the priest, misunderstood the intensity of her prayer. He thought she was drunk **(1 Sam. 1:13-14).**

Most of us women who are believers in Jesus Christ can recall or are now experiencing a barren or unfulfilled place in our lives too! No one has it all. I believe God allows it to be that way not because He gets some sort of thrill out of us not having what we long for, but He is lovingly guiding us to our created destiny, which is connected to the greater works of the salvation of Jesus.

"For the Lord hath called thee as a woman forsaken and grieved in spirit, and a wife of youth, when thou wast refused, saith thy God. For a small moment have I forsaken thee; but with great mercies will I gather thee. In a little wrath I hid my face from thee for a moment; but with everlasting kindness will I have mercy on thee, saith the Lord thy Redeemer.... -O thou afflicted, tossed with tempest, and not comforted, behold, I will lay thy stones with fair colours, and lay thy foundations with sapphires"(Is. 54:6-8, 11).

Living by faith can really take you through. It can be very natural just to go with what we see, but faith working from a genuine word from God will have you up at night. An authentic word from the Lord will cause you to pray over it, over and over; meditate on it, study and have it watered in fellowship wanting to know who can I talk to about it, as Mary did with Elizabeth **(Luke 1:39-45)**, because the Word of God is alive **(Heb. 4).**

Receiving a word or promise from God will require work. It will work you. Ask Joseph **(Gen. 37-50).** The hardest part is waiting as situations have a tendency to look, feel and become more and more hopeless. We may get nervous and anxious, but God is not nervous. He is not in Heaven biting His nails wondering,"How I am going to do this?"

Sarai had waited so long that she just did not believe the birth of a child could possibly happen through her and began concocting her own plan to bring about God's will through her servant Hagar*(Gen. 16)*. This only created more problems, heartache and grief.

You Are Going to Have This Baby!

That's how the devil does, same old stuff. He works to bring doubt into our hearts about the very will of God that we know! Then the devil gives his direction on how we should do it. That's why we have to take the time to pray *(No way around it)*. He did it with Eve in the garden. "...hath God said, Ye shall not eat of every tree of the garden **(Gen. 3:1)?** Even with the very Son of God, "...If thou be the Son of God, command this stone that it be made bread"**(Lk. 4:3).** Where Jesus responds with the word **(Eph. 6:17** *the sword of the Spirit),*"...

> "It is written, that man shall not live by bread alone, but by every word of God"**(Lk. 4:4).**

We too must be ready to respond with the word of God.

After waiting so long, not only did Sarai began to doubt and to conclude this promise would not come through her but so did Abraham. He went along with Sarai's plan. Isn't it funny *(peculiar)* that just when we have put our plan, our alternative plan to fulfill God's will, into action, He shows up. God speaks to Abram in **Genesis 17**, changing his name to Abraham and then announces to him Sarai's new name, Sarah **(Gen. 17:15).** I have not found where God changed any other woman's name in the Bible, maybe there is but I couldn't find it. God used Sarah in such a way then that even today she is a mentor to women and particularly married women. She stands out.

Where Abraham doubted that Sarah would produce a son and Sarah doubted herself, God shows up and brings her right back into the picture, right back to the uncomfortable place of the impossible*(faith).* We find that God first deals with Abraham alone regarding the promised child that would come through Sarah.

Look at Abraham's initial response to this news in **Gen. 17:17-18,** he falls on his face, and laughs."How could I become a father at the age of 100?" he thought. "And how can Sarah have a baby when she is ninety years old?" **Gen. 17-16-21** tells the story:

> 16 And I will bless her, and give thee a son also of her: yea, I will bless her, and she shall be a mother of nations; kings of people shall be of her.

Michele Smith

17 Then Abraham fell upon his face, and laughed, and said in his heart, Shall a child be born unto him that is a hundred years old? and shall Sarah, that is ninety years old, bear?

18 And Abraham said unto God, O that Ishmael might live before thee!

19 And God said, Sarah thy wife shall bear thee a son indeed; and thou shalt call his name Isaac: and I will establish my covenant with him for an everlasting covenant, and with his seed after him.

20 And as for Ishmael, I have heard thee: Behold, I have blessed him, and will make him fruitful, and will multiply him exceedingly; twelve princes shall he beget, and I will make him a great nation.

21 But my covenant will I establish with Isaac, which Sarah shall bear unto thee at this set time in the next year.

Then not long after that encounter with the Lord, he experiences another one in **Genesis 18.** The Lord visits Abraham's dwelling place among a party of three men, and declared again that Sarah would have a son. This time she hears it too being in the tent door **(vs. 9)** and laughs, with an attitude of, "Yeah, right!" Here God questions her laughing and she lies. So He challenges her faith here with the question, Is any thing too hard for the Lord" **(Gen. 18:14)?**Whew! What an encounter!

When God is purposing to do something special through your life, don't be too disturbed if you find yourself alone like Abraham. Know that as God calls you, He will also bless and increase you. Your latter will be greater. Here we see Him bringing hope back. Making it very clear she would give birth. It was not what she had concocted through Hagar her servant for the promise given to them years before.

He comes reassuring us of His promises. I know I received the Lord's firm assurance that my desire to encourage others, to write and counsel, doing work I love, would come to pass.

When I began to ponder how I was getting older and had veered off course, I thought about the things I would hear other older people saying; "Child that's for these young people…"

60

You Are Going to Have This Baby!

Some would start to live their hopes through their children. God immediately arrested my thinking and encouraged me through His word that He was going to do it through me, Hallelujah! Not through my children, not people I admire or mentored, but through me.

So I received the Lord saying clearly to me, "You are going to have this baby *(vision)*," just as He reassured Abraham and Sarah.

"And he said, I will certainly return unto thee according to the time of life; and, lo, Sarah thy wife shall have a son...."**(Gen. 18:10).**

I praise God for leading us through His word, confirming His promises to us and removing doubt. That is one of the wonderful things about being in a relationship and not just being religious. We can count on Him.

We can stand on that word He speaks to our heart, and it will hold up when the winds and waves come barreling in all around, when others doubt and even when we doubt ourselves.

I appreciate Him so much because He really doesn't have to do this, but He is such a loving Father that He does. The following are scriptures in which He began to speak to my spirit, passages that encouraged me so much when I really needed them. I pray that they would be rhema and encouragement for those who need them too, right now! When God does this, we like Abraham can exemplify great faith **(Rom. 4:20).**

"Through faith also Sara herself received strength to conceive seed, and was delivered of a child when she was past age, because she judged him faithful who had promised"**(Heb. 11:11).**

Another thing we can learn as we look to Abraham and Sarah **(Is. 51:2).** This is also what they failed to do at their point of weariness in waiting for the promise. "Call unto me, and I will answer thee, and show thee great and mighty things, which thou knowest not"**(Jer. 33:3).** We want to be sure that we do this.

There is nothing in all the world like a word from the Lord to help and encourage as we journey through this world with the many natural circumstances, setbacks and doubters that say the things we hope and dream for cannot happen. Thank God for His mercy in spite of our failure to cry out to Him when we should. These things can easily steer us off the course of our destination or destiny, but then God shows up and is faithful to finish the work He has begun in us. We need only believe and ask when we don't know the next move or when we have come to the end of our own knowledge of a thing.

Believers who live without the knowledge of God's word for themselves can easily end up chasing fantasies or false hope, carrying out fleshly methods to acquire the plan of God for our lives. Sarah and Abraham did and ended up with unplanned hardship. Remember their example. Leaning on God and learning to enjoy where we are, which I'll quickly admit is much easier said than done, is essential. There is incredible victory and the deeper things of the Lord some get to experience but many of us may miss. Yet what is encouraging and consoling to know is that wherever you are in your life's journey if you have missed it, know that Jesus Christ is the God of the second chance and your new day can start right now!

Just turn with humility and an honest heart and confess it to Jesus, who is the Second Chance, over and over again. God has made provision because He knows that often we may not get it all immediately, rarely is it instantaneous, more often, it's progressive, as we learn and grow in our relationship with Him. So let's remember to ask the Lord, for He is ready and willing to give us and make known to us great and mighty things. It is absolutely His good pleasure to do so.

The Kingdom of God offers so much to us. When we belong to Him, our borders are expanded. Salvation through Jesus Christ is just the beginning of the many things available to the believer for the fulfillment of purpose and for His glory. God is so intricately involved in the development of our lives; He is the Author and Finisher of our faith **(Heb. 12:2)**, and Oh my, the extent to which He will go to show us, when we are willing to get out of the boat and trust Him.

Testimony

One personal experience I can recall of God developing my faith and keeping me rightly aligned was during my pregnancy with my fifth and

You Are Going to Have This Baby!

youngest child at age 39. I was a nervous mess. At a time when I was looking forward to branching out in service to the Lord and ministry, our youngest at that time, Malachi who was well into school age and doing well. So this was very trying for me approaching 40; I thought why couldn't I do like everyone else turning 40 and just have a party?

Tragic Event, God's Mercy

I learned a very valuable and costly lesson after the conception of my second child, Abigail, whom I aborted. Immediately following the procedure, I experienced the emptiness, conviction, loss and grief as I realized I had allowed the life in me that I was supposed to protect and nurture to be ended through abortion because of fear, pride, humiliation and selfishness. The world's way of doing things is very deceptive.

I tried to clean up the mess I was making of my life at that time during a repeated course of bad relationships, while I was frantically searching for true love.

"I charge you, O ye daughters of Jerusalem, by the roes, and by the hinds of the field, that ye stir not up, nor awake my love, till he please" **(Song of Solomon 2:7).**

Though I was certainly saved, I was very naive and lost. And was unable to be honest with myself without God's Word, I wasn't facing the truth, I was looking for it. I had left my childhood church fellowship at nineteen, not knowing where to find it or rather Him but just innately knowing that there had to be more to this Jesus, than what I was experiencing. In spite of my ignorance and poor choices, the Lord was there for me, uncondemning, in love. He brought me through to truth, forgiveness and healing later to share my testimony with many, then on to counseling other young women in a crisis or unexpected pregnancy. *(God can and will speak to an ignorant mind that sincerely wants to do what is right),*

After I had become pregnant with my fifth child, during a financially trying time for us, I knew that abortion was not an option. Even though a close family member who was saved too suggested it.

A few days after that conversation, the top-notch doctor who was head of an OB/GYN, pediatrics department.

Actually reprimanded me for waiting so long to get a checkup *(I was in denial for four months)*.

Although I was an emotional wreck, with God's word in me arose courage through which I responded calmly yet firmly , that even if something was wrong with my baby, abortion was not an option!

Divine Connections

A woman of God, Rev. Patricia encouraged me in God's word, reminding me of the His impeccable and unmatchable character, that He would be there for me.

"Shall I bring to the birth, and not cause to bring forth? saith the Lord: shall I cause to bring forth, and shut the womb? saith thy God" **(Isaiah 66:9).**

She further began to speak prophetically through this word and referred to a spiritual birthing of ministry. God had a purpose through my life of worship and prayer (intercession) to preach the Gospel of Jesus Christ.

So, Who Are You? What's God's Plan?

Here it is! Very simple, just fill in the blank . *Here are a few Bible examples:*

- **Paul,** "...an apostle, (not of men, neither by man, but by Jesus Christ, and God the Father, who raised him from the dead;")**(Gal. 1:1).**

- **James,** "a servant of God and of the Lord Jesus Christ..."**(Jam. 1:1).**
- **Peter,** "an apostle of Jesus Christ,"**(1 Pet. 1:1).**
- **Deborah,** "a prophetess, the wife of Lapidoth"**(Jdg. 4:4).**
- **Miriam,** "the prophetess, the sister of Aaron,"**(Ex. 15:20).**
- **Luke,** "the beloved physician,"**(Col. 4:14).**
- **THOSE WOMEN,** "which laboured with me in the gospel..."**(Phil.4:3).**

You Are Going to Have This Baby!

Your Name: ───────────────

Your God Ordained Purpose Or Calling:

───────────────────

Your Occupation:

─────────────────────────

Encouragement

If completing this brief statement causes you to be sad, afraid or bewil- dered; or if you're saying, "I've never really thought about it. I just do what I have to do" that's a lot of us.

Declare this as day one, a new day where you allow God to bring you clarity of purpose and into your divine destiny. This in no way is meant to get anyone caught up in self-centeredness and pride in the calling of God but to encourage you to embrace the plan of God for you and not miss it, living an aimless, powerless life.

He came for us to live much more than that **(Jn. 10:10)**, not just fluff and puff. Then your life can send a message of hope and encouragement to others with or without words **(1 Pet. 3:1)**. Are you able to say in one or two sentences who you are?

Minister Omar Barlow ministered a powerfully stirring and prophetic word regarding God knowing us before we were formed in the womb from **Jer. 1:5** and pointing out the sad reality that many living on this earth, leave this world a mystery to themselves and everybody around them. Nobody really knew who they were.

That word pushed me forward. I challenge you to let it be evident, the witness of Christ and God's kingdom work in and through your life. Receive the ultimate reward of hearing God say to you, "...Well done, good and faithful servant;..."**(Mt. 25:23)**.

Jesus Christ Example for Us

Remember the response of the centurion when Jesus died on the cross yielding up His spirit **(Mt. 27:50)**.

65

He understood what Jesus had come for. He said, "Truly this was the Son of God" **(Mt. 27:54).** I want to send out a blast and provoke something in you even as I challenge myself. I want God's best for my life, not the cookie cutter models the world is manufacturing, a life of mediocrity. I don't want to miss it, nor do I want to see anyone else who desires God's best for her or his life to miss it either. The world is waiting, **(Rom. 8:19)** so be led by the Spirit, and give God the place to show you some things, vital things you may not know **(Jer. 33:3).** He knows the latter end and it will be greater. He wants to increase us more and more, our children too. Go ahead, have your baby, your Isaac (laughter)! And we can laugh with Him.

"He that sitteth in the heavens shall <u>laugh...</u>" **(Ps 2:4)**

God's Command to the Husband

God instructs the husband to love his wife as Christ loves the church: **Ephesians 5:25-31**

> 25 Husbands, love your wives, even as Christ also loved the church, and gave himself for it;

> 26 That he might sanctify and cleanse it with the washing of water by the word,

> 27 That he might present it to himself a glorious church, not having spot, or wrinkle, or any such thing; but that it should be holy and without blemish.

> 28 So ought men to love their wives as their own bodies. He that loveth his wife loveth himself.

> 29 For no man ever yet hated his own flesh; but nourisheth and cherisheth it, even as the Lord the church:

> 30 For we are members of his body, of his flesh, and o his bones.

> 31 For this cause shall a man leave his father and mother, and shall be joined unto his wife, and they two shall be one flesh

So ladies, let's look here, and do a little dissecting of this passage from the Bible. Why? So that we will have hope and know how we should pray so that we are in line with God's heart and will for our marriage relationship and so that we can become genuine witnesses of Christ and the church to the world.

In the beginning of marriage, most of the time we *(both husband & wife)* put our best foot forward. That's when things are easy, love and romance, special attention, acts of kindness— until the newness wears off and conflict , offenses, familiarity, then disappointment arise. These toxins invade the love flow and intimacy. If left unattended and unresolved, they will corrode the relationship.

"Be ye angry, and sin not: let not the sun go down on your wrath"**(Eph. 4:26).**

God's Command to the Husband

Forgiveness is huge and selflessness, as so beautifully demonstrated by our Savior, Jesus Christ at Calvary. This is the model that God is requiring here in the command to husbands to love their wives.

When any of us experiences God's unconditional love, then we can properly demonstrate love and forgiveness to others. God did this for us through His own Son, whose life He gave up for our sins, taking away our spots and wrinkles. So, as we choose through faith in Christ to forgive one another, we will wash away those toxins and allow for a cleansing, refreshing, renewal and a stronger relationship.

When I consider how *Christ loves His Church (to me & you)*, and think of words to describe, I choose: Selflessly, Sacrificially, expensively, including, tenderly leading, kindly teaching, intimate conversation, listening, covering and providing; strong and protecting but not inhibiting, gently guiding, guiding wisely, dying, saving, giving and forgiving. These are just some of the words that come to mind of Jesus' expressed love to the Church *(to me and you)*.

You can add some of your own. Please feel free to do so in the spaces here:

_____,_,

_____,_____,

_____,_____,

_____,_____,

This type of sacrificial love *(agape)* is huge and is contrary to our fallen human nature in which love usually has strings or conditions attached. It is impossible to demonstrate this type of love without the endowment of the Holy Spirit. As wives, understanding this shows us how we can pray, asking God's help to bring your husband into this kind of love, which is not natural but supernatural. Pray that your husband would have a personal experience of God's love for himself, and as he does, that it will overflow into your relationship and all that he does. God's love is powerful, very impactful and never failing.

"That He might sanctify and cleanse it with the washing of water by the word" **(Eph. 5:26).**

This refers to Christ's relationship to the Church and to the husband's relationship to the wife. Husbands, when you made vows to her during the wedding ceremony before guests and witnesses you promised to set your wife apart from all others*(...forsaking all others)*, and so as you are to walk in obedience to fulfill your promise*(vow)* to love. You are to give heed to Christ in His command and example. You cause spiritual cleansing in her life with your love and the word of God, to take away spots and wrinkles *(wounds & bruises)*, not add them.

"That He might present it to Himself a glorious church, not having spot or wrinkle or any such thing; but that it should be holy and without blemish" **(Eph. 5-27).**

Through your praying of the word, sharing, caring and demonstrating, she gets washed. That's what God's word does, bringing encouragement and value.

Because of this, things happen. She begins to blossom, and people will want to know who her husband is. As she flourishes in her commitment and care of the home, community and her life's work, she is presented to you! Your heart can be proud and the benefit, the favor of God's blessing your life, will be a powerful display of His glory. It will not have to be said she had to do it on her own, or that sister or brother so and so helped her. The accolades will come to you.

"So ought men to love their wives as their own bodies. He that loveth his wife loveth himself " **(Eph. 5:28).**

What godly woman wouldn't want to please a husband like that in every way? I'll answer, none. Remember, the state of any household is a direct reflection of its leadership. Be discerning of the stench that comes from the flesh and the devil: jealousy , deceit, wrath and pride.

Whether a man through Christ has gained a heart to love His wife or not, is in itself proof of whether or not he loves himself.

"For no man ever yet hated his own flesh; but nourisheth and cherisheth it, even as the Lord the church"**(Eph. 5:29).**

God's Command to the Husband

There is a picture of a true healthy man of God, how he treats his wife. She is even as his own flesh, the Bible says.

"And the Lord God caused a deep sleep to fall upon Adam, and he slept: and he took one of his ribs, and closed up the flesh instead thereof And the rib, which the Lord God had taken from man, made he a woman, and brought her unto the man" **(Gen. 2:21-22).**

"....a man leave his father and mother, and shall be joined unto his wife, and they two shall be one flesh" **(Eph. 5:30-31).**

Priority is clearly established here.
He who loves his wife loves himself, and there once again is a witness of Christ. This is a very beautiful thing and is encouraging to many.

Husbands should obey the command of God and so experience His blessings here in this life and the future rewards to come. Wonderful benefits come with being a loving and caring husband.

"Husbands, in the same way be considerate as you live with your wives, and treat them with respect as the weaker partner and as heirs with you of the gracious gift of life, so that nothing will hinder your prayers"**(1 Pet. 3:7).**

Loving his wife, it is a witness of Christ as well as his "reasonable service" because of God's mercy **(Rom. 12:1).**

Again, wives, understanding the huge responsibility that lies upon the shoulders of your husband should cause you to pray for him fervently, never take this for granted. Thank God continually if you have a husband who is displaying this type of quality and share encouragement and pray with those who are not. Thank God and pray continually if your husband is not living up to this that he'll do so and receive God's rich rewards and that your lives together can be a witness. Greater is He that is in you, so declare God's blessing over your husband, take authority over the kingdom of darkness!

"I pray the Lord will minister to you regarding your marriage relationship and enrich your lives more and more, your and your children eve to "a thousand generations"(Deut. 7:9), in Jesus Name, Amen.

God's Command to the Wife

"Wives, submit yourselves unto your own husbands, as unto the Lord" **(Eph. 5:22)**.

In the previous chapter, we looked to the scripture dealing with God's command to the husband regarding his wife, which actually come after the verses directed to the wife. I did it this way for few reasons:

1. For wives to have a fresh realization of God's expectation of a husband's treatment of you, his wife.

2. To invoke compassion in us wives because of the huge weight of responsibility our husbands may feel and so move us to pray more fervently for God's wisdom, revelation and grace for our husbands.

3. Most important for vision, to gain a healthy perspective from God's viewpoint of what the marriage relationship should look like.

"Where there is no vision, the people perish: but he that keepeth the law, happy is he" **(Prv. 29:18)**.

Some readers may not know what this is supposed to look like. Many of you might have come from backgrounds of abuse, broken relationships, poor behavior and/or dysfunctions in your upbringing that contributed to what we mostly see now. Sadly in our nation so many homes are fatherless and in some cases motherless too. Now, unless someone points people to what the Bible says about our Creator's purpose and intent, we may very well be responsible for perpetuating perversions of the world systems and strategies.

We have covered quite a bit on the wife's role of submitting to her own husband. The main emphasis of this chapter is to recognize that this is God's *command* not a suggestion. We all have a debt to pay and that debt is love **(Rom. 13:8)**. It is also to implore you to go back to the Word of God regarding this important topic and review, meditate and pray. Courageously examine yourself, ask whether you are obeying or maybe falling short in some area.

Some of us will have to dust off that Bible sitting on the coffee table or

God's Command to the Wife

mantle in our homes with pages that have changed colors because you keep it opened to familiar parts. Now, you may find you have a quickening desire to read on to provoke fresh conversation between you and your Lord. He loves us so much, He's not condemning. It's our own disobedience to Him, which may just be from a lack of knowledge that condemns us, "My people are destroyed for lack of knowledge..." **(Hos. 4:6).**

God is so good, and He wants us to get it right. He personally wants to wash us and does so with His word because He is for us living a rich and fulfilled life.

"...If I wash thee not, thou hast no part with me"**(Jn. 13:8).**
"Now ye are clean through the word which I have spoken unto you"**(Jn.15:3).**

O sisters, God takes a special interest in you and me as He does all the body of Christ. You don't have to wait for your husband. When you're already aware you have an area in your life that's stinking, wash yourself with the word. Get in Bible Study with other women who are sincere and caring, who are also working to grow in the holiness of God themselves or just to get wisdom **(Jam. 1:5)** or seek out godly counsel from someone trustworthy who's walking in truth.

Most importantly, get in the presence of God, worship Him and get His attention for revelation and inspiration.

In **Ephesians 5:22-24** are just some of the scripture references in which we are given God's command as married women. You can cross-reference and find other .

We must obey God's command if we want to see and experience great results in our lives.

Sisters, I know this is hard for many who have been abused or neglected *(another form of abuse).* For those who have suffered betrayal, oppression, abandonment and devastation, the word of God offers hope for the healing of families, communities and nations.

We have to begin individually and remain determined to wrestle through these areas in prayer and rise up having heard from the Lord, prepared to carry out His instructions for the rich and fulfilled life Jesus promised in **(John 10:10)**. This longing and desire develop as you cultivate your relationship with the Lord. No one can force this on you, but when you embrace it, it will bless your life and transform you family.

God does not force you into this. That's why the Bible says. "...Many are called, but few are chosen"**(Mat. 22:14).** You have to want it badly enough that you're willing to pay the price.

Many years ago, when I was challenged with the idea of submission, I was horrified and didn't want really to entrust myself and my happiness to anyone. I felt the need to have control, but God was showing me something different.

"He must increase, but I must decrease" **(Jn. 3:30).**

This is what I kept hearing in my spirit.

Testimony

One time I sensed a particular direction I felt God was leading us to go for our marriage and for our family. I wanted to say something to my husband so badly, but God wasn't permitting me to. I was yielding and praying fervently. Just when I thought it would just spill out of my mouth, my husband walks in the kitchen, looks at me and begins speaking to me regarding that very matter. I was floored, amazed and so grateful to learn how God was there with me working in my husband's heart as I humbly submitted to His word and His leading.

He was very present and helping because our marriage was being challenged. God was there, loving and guiding us both. I was sensing in a great way His arms around us, and I was encouraged all the more, desiring to let go and trust Him.

Testimony and confirmation of God's direction in learning submission.

Several years ago, my friend Alberta, a dear woman of God, and I had agreed, as we both felt led by the Lord, to meet early on Sunday mornings at the altar to worship and pray before service. This meant I needed to get up

God's Command to the Wife

even earlier to have my private time at home, to hear from the Lord, tune in and submit my life to Him in a fresh way. What I received at this time from the Lord were three words, "Just obey Him." Well, I responded all excited, "Yes, Lord! Hallelujah! I delight to do Your will, Father. My heart's desire is to glorify Your name." I bowed in worship and humble submission, my answer was "Yes!"

When I got to the church to meet Alberta, she was already there in prayer, and I joined in. Well, following our time in the Lord's Presence came the confirmation. Alberta began sharing with me that she had purchased several books and had just given one to a friend of hers. It was titled "Just Obey Him." Very excited, I responded, "Oh my, I need that book." I shared with her the word the Lord had just spoken to me.

After service, she went to her car, came over and handed me the book with the title, "Just Obey him" with a little "h," and my response was, "obey him!"

Boy, was I shaking, my insides all twisted and flopping up and down. My neck was loose and rotating. What! I was in trouble because the Lord was speaking. Earlier I was thinking, "Oh yes, I'll obey You, Jesus, yes, but wait a minute, are You telling me to obey him? Oh God, but nevertheless not my will, Lord, but Yours."

Now I am not at all saying that he was bad. My husband is a wonderful man, intelligent, humble and a faithful provider who loves the Lord. Yet the contrasts of our backgrounds were so great. I come from a very sheltered environment where my mother and father were present and involved. I played right at home with siblings in the backyard, and I didn't feel I was missing anything.

My husband grew up very young in street life after his parents broke up. His mother, as many single parents did, worked many years trying to do the work that God intended to be done through two people. I knew that troubled my husband's heart deeply as he felt her struggle, pain and tears.

I'm the type who likes to dip my toes in the water slowly to get used to the water temperature. My husband would jump right in and wade in the water. He likes a lot of noise, I like quiet. He had such a free spirit with a lot fewer restrictions.

Oh my, what a faith walk of having to put myself daily on the altar and die to the self-life, yielding to God in respecting my husband's headship, in other words, calling him "lord." This was excruciating, but at the same time wonderful, because once I submitted and got my flesh out of the way I was able to experience the Lord and that's priceless, living and learning to develop eyes to see, having that single eye **(Mt. 6:22)**.

I was looking not to the things I could see, touch, taste and feel *(natural senses)*, but to the unseen *(spiritual senses)*. I was learning to walk in the Spirit where the true realities of Christ are and looking from God's viewpoint instead of my own, which might have me in the center instead of Him.

God was teaching me about not being fearful or struck with amazement **(1 Peter 3:6)** of what seemed out of my control, and bringing my emergencies to Him. I was learning to remain calm in my faith and trust in Him.

He was teaching me secrets, unfolding the mystery of the true position of power, authority and beauty as a wife, the beauty of Christ radiating out of my life. He wanted my life lived to please Him and to be a model before my husband to behold for the hope and possibility of his being won over without the word **(1 Peter 3:1)**, or me preaching to him.

Especially as I conducted small meetings in my home, reaching out to women with questions, women in crisis needing God's help and to learn God's way, my own life would be an example to them as well. I called these home meetings" Sarah Daughters" as the Lord had originally spoken to me some 19 years before in North Carolina.

Remember the admonishment of God to those following after righteousness **(Is. 51:2)** to look at Sarah's life as well as Abraham's. Look to women like her, holy women of old **(1 Pet. 3:5)**. Take note here when God was referring to a disobedient spouse, He was talking about Abraham. Now that threw me a bit, father of faith Abraham? Then the Lord reminded me that He speaks the end from the beginning.

"(As it is written, I have made thee a father of many nations,) before him whom he believed, even God, who quickeneth the dead, and calleth those things which be not as though they were"**(Rom. 4:17)**.

God's Command to the Wife

Here is our example to follow, dear sisters! When we do not obey God's command, it brings into question whether our love for Him is genuine, it robs us of the opportunity of being a witness of Christ in the earth, and most importantly, of God of His glory. We can grieve our Heavenly Father who is like us as parents but on a much higher level of perfection, and delights to prosper His little ones, His bride who we are.

I'm not talking about an occasional missing of the mark, but a set pattern of disobedience that results in a marred believer who needs to go back to the Potter's house for a work over. He is the Husbandman who is coming for His Bride *(the Church, the Body of Christ)* to be made ready, without spot or wrinkle.

Sadly, some may never get it, and they will be surprised when they find themselves having to answer to God regarding their disobedience to His commands on that appointed day, and submission is one of the commands. Of course, we have no control over the will of our spouse and their choices.

Each of us has been given a free will to choose to obey or not, accept what God commands or reject it. So we can choose to obey God, but we can't choose for someone else. What we can do is pray and live as a godly example before them and when given opportunity, share Christ's saving grace.

Obedience does not assure we won't have hardship, but remember the sufferings we endure for Christ cannot compare to the rich rewards that will be ours to come **(Rom. 8:18).**

Important Question:
Is there ever a time not to submit to your husband?

Well, looking to Sarah, by whom the general standard of righteousness is set, thinking of just her scenario, I might say, "No." Then, as I look at some of the other holy women of old that Peter speaks about **(1 Pet. 3:5),** I would say yes there is.

The Bible gives examples of wise, courageous and discerning women of faith who in important instances knew what to do and understood timing and opportunity, whose husband's trusted them. They were women like the Shunammite **(2 Kings 4:22-23),** like Abigail **(1 Sam. 25:19)** and Esther whose husband was the King **(Est. 4:16).** They were women who lived by the leading of the Lord. Their intent even in challenges was to do good and not harm to their husbands **(Prv. 31:12).**

Being a wife who submits does not mean you don't use your own mind. One example that says there are occasions not to obey or submit is seen in the terrible fate of Sapphira who husband's name was Ananias. She was privy to her husband's scheme to sell land but lied about the price, costing both their lives.

"Then Peter said unto her, How is it that ye have agreed together to tempt the Spirit of the Lord? behold, the feet of them which have buried thy husband are at the door, and shall carry thee out"**(Acts 5:9).**

So the answer is yes.

It's all about authority. Remember the centurion whose servant was sick in **Mt. 8:5-10.** He understood authority, and Jesus marveled.

"For I am a man under authority, having soldiers under me: and I say to this man, Go, and he goeth; and to another, Come, and he cometh; and to my servant, Do this, and he doeth it. When Jesus heard it, he marvelled, and said to them that followed, Verily I say unto you, I have not found so great faith, no, not in Israel" **(Mt. 8:9-10).**

The point is he had an understanding of rank and submission in the natural carnal world and how they worked together. More than anything, he had grasped the principal and recognized a Higher Heavenly authority was present.

So grasping the purpose of submission and the order of how God has set the family, while steadfastly trusting God, is so valuable. It sets the stage for miracles, powerful displays of God's glory.

In short, dear beautiful sisters in Christ,
Just obey HIM

Divided Devotions?

"But I would have you without carefulness. He that is unmarried careth for the things that belong to the Lord, how he may please the Lord: But he that is married careth for the things that are of the world, how he may please his wife. There is a difference also between a wife and a virgin. The unmarried woman careth for the things of the Lord, that she may be holy both in body and in spirit: but she that is married careth for the things of the world, how she may please her husband. And this I speak for your own profit; not that I may cast a snare upon you, but for that which is comely, and that ye may attend upon the Lord without distraction"**(1 Cor. 7:32-35).**

When I first read this passage, I was perplexed about the boundaries of being wholly devoted to God and pleasing my husband, considering how different our levels of conviction and commitment were. The Lord only allowed me to realize who my husband was when I was completely sold out to Him at age 31, though He had initially introduced us to one another as teenagers. I believe a major reason God made me wait was that because in my emotional state of mind, I surely would have put my husband in the place of God, having him up on a pedestal.

I am so happy to know that as I am submitting to my husband and respecting him, I am really submitted to Christ. My husband Andrew, is a man of God who so longs after God. However, when I began to feel a certain distancing in our relationship and an emotional disconnect because of our personality differences, childhood backgrounds and choice of friends, I became very insecure. I had to fight not to fall under the oppressive feeling of being devalued.

Earlier on, through a desperate need to be in right standing with God, I had come to total surrender in my Christian walk at age 31. A little less than a year later, I was divinely reconnected to this man who would be my husband, a man whose face would often pleasantly come to mind, though I had not seen him for over 14 years. When we met in our teens, what developed was a fondness of one another. I always hoped nothing but the best for him and he always had pleasantly thought of me, as my sisters would tell me when they saw him.

Divided Devotions?

I think it was mutual though that we didn't feel very compatible to one another.

The End and the Beginning

At age 30, I joined a healthy church body in which I started learning about the Baptism of the Holy Spirit and the evidence. The Bible Study was very rich. I began to grow in leaps and bounds in knowledge and experience profound revelation. My hunger, my appetite for the Lord, His Word and His Presence became insatiable. I believe the Lord was excited for me, like Moses at the burning bush. I was finally captured and seeking Him as never before. He knew I was searching before, and though it was for the right things, it was in the wrong ways.

Jesus Christ began revealing Himself to me, and in me, and my journey of faith had become so awesome. I had discovered that no one else could ever satisfy or compare.

After responding to a continuous urging that I had for years to go away from everything I was familiar with, I finally took a mad leap of faith. I had a desperate desire to begin walking sincerely in the principles of the Bible I had begun learning. I was so hungry to know things about God I had never known before and that was my prayer. Holiness became my unending quest because I wanted to please the Lord who had been so good to me in spite of myself and of my bloopers and blunders, I realized He is my sure help.

Before then, my life was in a constant cycle of failure and disappointment in myself and in others. I had managed to make a mess out of my life. I hated being here in this cruel, cold and uncaring world, as I fell into periods of hopelessness and despair I would cry out to God, "What am I here for?" Thank God for Jesus Christ, who became so real in my life. I desperately wanted change.

Transformation, which seemed an impossible thing because of the oppression and the environment I had lived in and my own weakness to sin. I realized the devil doesn't play games, and I wasn't trying to play any either. I had come to understand he was strong on his agenda to destroy my life, my seed *(godly offspring)* and others.

At my total surrender, I had entrusted my all to the Lord, including my desire for love and family, now my focus and attention was upon Him. Thank God, the yoke of the devil *(ungodly ties)* was broken. The compulsive urge to bring about God's will my way was removed, and I was liberated. I was finally at the end of me, and I built an altar to the Lord and named it, "The Place Where I Died." I began daily seeking first God's' kingdom for real this time, as well as His wisdom and righteousness, listened intently for His counsel.

Not long after that, God began revealing His will for me in this area of ministry, in marriage and family. I moved from North Carolina back to Pennsylvania. My first evening back there was a knock at the door. It was Andrew, my childhood interest. After not seeing or hearing from him for about 14 years, we were reconnected and soon wed.

Two years into our marriage, God began to speak to me about "Sarah's daughters," which brought me to an in-depth home Bible study *(what we call a cell or life group)*. We studied the holy women of old, taking a finer look at Sarah, the wife of Abraham, one of our Patriarchs.

God was equipping me for success, giving me his design for being a godly wife, a woman of virtue, professing holiness and accepting my proper role in marriage to honor Him. He was giving me understanding and a path to avoid the perplexity of many women who when called into ministry make poor or badly timed decisions.

Apostle Paul writes, "Andthis I speak for your own profit; not that I may cast a snare upon you, but for that which is comely, and that ye may attend upon the Lord without distraction"(**1 Cor. 7:35).**

Trick of the Devil

From my own experience, I know the devil likes to add anxiety, anguish and torment to the lives of single women who love God and serve Him. He tries to make us think that if we don't have the love of a good man, a ring on our finger and a wedding date set that something's wrong with us. The devil is a liar! If we listen to this, we can miss contentment and joy in our lives. We can fall into the temptation of doing things out of time, but God is there to give us assurance of His plan for our lives and peace, by way of His Spirit, the Holy Ghost, Glory!

Divided Devotions?

"For God hath not given us the spirit of fear; but of power, and of love, and of a sound mind"(**2 Tim. 1:7**).

"Be careful for nothing; but in every thing by prayer and supplication with thanksgiving let your requests be made known unto God"**(Phil. 4:6)**.

As married women, we struggle to balance our family life and ministry, so that we do not take our husbands for granted and neglect our home, especially when we have small children. As we run about to all kinds of conferences, seminars and church meetings, the devil likes to bring anxiety and confusion. We can become resentful, bitter, discontented and so tempted to do things out of season. I have experienced both struggles and have cried out to the Lord in my dilemma. He answers, giving me assurance of His plan for me, with this comes much joy and peace. So remember in times like these where our peace is challenged:

God is available and invites us to call on Him in these tempting situations.

"Call unto me, and I will answer thee, and show thee great and mighty things, which thou knowest not" **(Jer. 33:3)**.

"Trust in him at all times; ye people, pour out your heart before him: God is a refuge for us. Selah"**(Ps. 62:8)**.

So God has given both his promise and his oath.

"That by two immutable things, in which it was impossible for God to lie, we might have a strong consolation, who have fled for refuge to lay hold upon the hope set before us:"**(Heb. 6:18)**.

We can count on Him, and that's reason for praise.

There it is, sisters. It can be tough at times, but righteousness delivers us. We are serving the Lord as we embrace submission, respecting our husbands, yet always ready to do good and not live in fear. It is definitely a faith walk, and as the Lord's servants, we build our homes when we embrace God's wisdom. We tear it down when we give way to our fears, not trusting God completely.

We set the atmosphere in our homes positively when with a quiet spirit we get to our own quiet place and worship. We get answers for our needs and emergencies. We affect it negatively when we are shaken with fear and don't shut down that impulse to be in control when we feel we can perceive the outcome of our husband's actions that he may not see or we don't have enough details about how God may be leading him.

Picture yourself in Sarah's situation, when the chosen man of God announces, "We've got to pack up and leave here because God said..."**(Gen. 12:1).**

You ask, "Well where are we going?" He says, "I don't know." Can you see this?

Or, your husband says something like this, "Well, let's go to Egypt, but tell them you're my sister **(Gen. 12:12-13)**, as Abraham asked Sarah to do for his protection. OK?

So like Abraham when, your husband is afraid, not operating in faith and coming up with his own ideas. Do you say, "Oh my Lord, if the head where the eyes *(vision, leadership, protection, covering)* and mouth *(declaring, life giving speech)* has lost touch, what do we do?" Here again we have the *word of God!*

"If the foundations be destroyed, what can the righteous do? The Lord is in his holy temple, the Lord's throne is in heaven: his eyes behold, his eyelids try, the children of men **(Ps. 11:3-4).**

That is what we women have to know, regardless of what storm comes, no matter how severe. We are on this boat *(in the home)* and Jesus is too, even if He appears to be in the "hinder part of the ship" asleep, He's got us **(Mk. 4:38-39)!** Better than that, He's in us and because of that we can with assurance let the humble and meek attitude of Christ set the tone in our homes **(1 Pet. 3:1).** We can declare peace and cause the course of events to be stilled.

"And David said to Abigail, Blessed be the Lord God of Israel, which sent thee this day to meet me: And blessed be thy advice, and blessed be thou, which hast kept me this day from coming to shed blood, and from avenging myself with mine own hand"**(1 Sam. 25:32-33).**

Divided Devotions?

When adversity comes in marriage, remember God has given us something the world calls "intuition" (Let's call it a special kind of discernment) so we know things, dear women of God, Eve knew about God and wanted to be like Him, Sarah knew that she and Abraham were to have a son, Rebecca knew that of her twin sons Jacob would carry on the line from which would come our Savior **(Gen. 25-23).**

We are God's secret weapon for our husbands, though sometimes grossly overlooked and unappreciated. My God wants us to learn more, connect and help each other in the rough times, to travail and gain the victory, instead of trying to accomplish what we know (God's very will) through our own methods.

Here is a clear example from which we can learn and find encouragement in Acts 27 regarding Paul's voyage to Rome, when the ship is tossed about by winds.

"And said unto them, Sirs, I perceive that this voyage will be with hurt and much damage, not only of the lading and ship, but also of our lives. Nevertheless the centurion believed the master and the owner of the ship, more than those things which were spoken by Paul"**(Acts. 27:10-11).** "But not long after there arose against it a tempestuous wind, called Euroclydon. And when the ship was caught, and could not bear up into the wind, we let her drive"**(Acts 14-15).**

"Which when they had taken up, they used helps, undergirding the ship; and, fearing lest they should fall into the quicksands, struck sail, and so were driven"**(Acts 27:17).**

They used ropes or "helps."
Ladies that us!

We must acquire understanding, know our position and not move from it, the only time we move, is if God says move, other than that we stand.

Michele Smith

"If the spirit of the ruler rise up against thee, leave not thy place; for yielding pacifieth great offences" **(Ecc. 10:4).**

Trust in God's power and timing, and commit to doing good. Remember the Greater One in us is greater than any challenge we'll ever face, to God be the glory! *(Abigail in 1 Samuel 25 is a great example of having understanding and knowing when to move).*

We must apply ourselves to the Word, precious sisters. Stay clothed in His righteousness and adorned in the beauty of meekness is of great price to God **(1 Pet. 3:4).** Paul makes it very plain as he writes that when we are living to please our husbands, we are also honoring the Lord, and He will look out for our best interest.

Again, we look at Paul's admonishment to the unmarried and the married, so that our devotions are not divided. We should each understand our role, appreciate one another, be encouraged and gain contentment when we are doing it with all our heart unto the Lord. God's word through both Peter and Paul (two key leading men of God) brings us back to the real focus, the ultimate goal and hope to bring an unbeliever to saving faith and the unbelieving back to faith in Christ. That is the unsaved and the backslider **(1 Pet. 3:1).**

This brings a healthy clarity to our role in the will and plan of God so there is no false guilt. As wives, we must care about the things of the world, giving proper attention to our earthly responsibilities to please our husbands. Though we may have great insight and revelation in the will of God, even then should we communicate that also with our husbands, as Manoah's wife did at the announcement of the birth of Samson, if they are open to listen.

"Then the woman came and told her husband, saying, A man of God came unto me, and his countenance was like the countenance of an angel of God, very terrible: but I asked him not whence he was, neither told he me his name: But he said unto me, Behold, thou shalt conceive, and bear a son; and now drink no wine nor strong drink, neither eat any unclean thing: for the child shall be a Nazarite to God from the womb to the day of his death" **(Judges 13:6-7).**

Divided Devotions?

Sometimes our husbands are not receptive for different reasons, for instance, if you have unresolved issues between the two of you, if he's been offended or if one of you is jealous.

Unlike Rebecca **(Gen. 27),** and her response though knowing God's will for her son Jacob, wanted to invest in that, but did it the wrong way. So, we too like Rebecca can feel the need to help God bring about his will even through deception and Sarai (Sarah)**(Gen. 16:1-3)** through using her maid Hagar to bring about the promised son. What did these women have in common? Fear.

All three woman encountered fear, Manoah's wife, Rebecca and Sarah but only one, Manoah's wife (who is never named in the Bible), was able to communicate and did good.

Marriage is more and more by the ways of the world, being perverted, degraded and taken way out of the original purpose God intended as antichrist spirits unfortunately work through our lawmakers. Through the agendas of those who have chosen to go their own way, working to intimidate believers into shutting down when we need to speak up.

The statistics of marriages in the church breaking down should be a wake up call to the church that more needs to be done than holding an annual marriage conference. The church needs to do more, in teaching, in support groups and open forums for singles and married people to interact, engage and learn.

When we are empowered with wisdom and knowledge, we can make better decisions. We can be inspired by hope, then many of the needs and problems tearing marriages apart and destroying them can be prevented. We can even save lives. This thing is so much bigger than we are. It's about God and what He is building, the Church.

Consider how the Holy Bible starts with marriage in Genesis and ends with marriage in Revelation.

"And Adam said, This is now bone of my bones, and flesh of my flesh: she shall be called Woman, because she was taken out of Man. Therefore shall a man leave his father and his mother, and shall cleave unto his wife: and they shall be one flesh **(Gen. 2:23-24).**

"And I John saw the holy city, new Jerusalem, coming down from God out of heaven, prepared as a bride adorned for her husband"**(Rev. 21:2).**

The Big Picture of Marriage

"This is a great mystery: but I speak concerning Christ and the church" **(Eph. 5:32).**

Calling Him "Lord"

"Even as Sara obeyed Abraham, calling him lord: whose daughters ye are, as long as ye do well, and are not afraid with any amazement"**(1 Pet. 3:6)**.

The use of this term did not necessarily mean that Sarah went around addressing her husband as "Lord this.." or "Lord that...." There was honor in the way she spoke of him. Her reference to him above as lord was in response to what she heard the *Lord say* **(Gen. 18: 10-15)**. This manner of reference points us to how we speak of our husbands to others and how we address him when we are around others. There is an heir of honor to be given here.

The term "lord" has a number of definition

lord – master (Source: http://dictionary.reverso.net)

1. a person who has power or authority over others, such as a monarch and master

2. a male member of the nobility, esp in Britain

3. Compare lady (in medieval Europe) a feudal superior, esp the master of a manor

4. a husband considered as head of the household (archaic except in the facetious phrase lord and master

This might just be me, but have you ever noticed that when some married women speak about their husbands, they often make sarcastic statements, complaints and jokes?

I have to confess that I have been guilty of and known of others who are guilty of joining in the flow of subtle slander and belittling. Some may say they really don't mean any harm and are just joining in the camaraderie of the work environment or social group setting. Then after we make remarks, we try to clean it up by saying something nice.

Calling Him "Lord"

Most of the time, the negative picture has already soothed the ears of those looking for faults.

This evidence clearly exposes the state of our hearts, and we need to take ownership of it and follow the path to healing. The prophet Jeremiah describes very plainly the state of the human heart that we should always consider and continually look to God to fill us and guide our lives.

"The heart is deceitful above all things, and desperately wicked: who can know it"**(Jer. 17:9)?**

Sometimes sadly, this is also true in women's ministry meetings or Bible studies and may reveal ministries or even churches born out of bitterness and resentment. We must be so careful to have the Lord often check us even after we've checked ourselves, which I know many do. For in this we can find help and healing.

"Search me, O God, and know my heart: try me, and know my thoughts: And see if there be any wicked way in me, and lead me in the way everlasting" **(Ps. 139:23-24).**

O what good medicine from the Lord!

God's word clearly directs in **Ephesians 5:33** for the wife to reverence her husband.

Disrespect for the spouse is not exclusive to women. We have seen or heard of married men, talking in the gym, workplace or other social settings, referring to their wives in derogatory terms like the "ball and chain," or sometimes much worse. We have to realize that when any of us as believers in Christ are doing this, it destroys our witness of Christ to one another and the world.

It is not that we can't vent, "be real" and share some of the hurts or disappointments, but we must be careful of how, when, where and with whom we are unpacking these things. God's word says to be careful that we don't devour one another **(Gal. 5:15).** The devil loves it, and you'll have no problem finding others who will quickly feed into the negative conversation. You are sure to get a crowd.

If you are doing things God's way, honoring your husband whether he is obeying the Word or not **(1 Pet. 3:1),** you'll find that the crowd will thin out.

Support Groups

You must choose a right place and time to get real matters out on the table and find a resolution. Otherwise, it is like letting a fire burn within no extinguisher to put it out, so it's inevitable that we have break ups and breakdowns. It is apparent that the fiery trials of marriage are at an all time high. troublesome times are here **(2 Tim. 3:1).**

It's very important for married couples to have safe places to learn, to be encouraged in righteousness and to vent frustration or concern so that they don't feel invisible, trapped and hopeless because they're hurting.

It's a constant cycle of failure if we don't up the ante. We need the type of support structure that will work on the preventive side of the conflict to save as many marriages and families as possible.

The Bible says,
"Confess your faults one to another, and pray one for another, that ye may be healed...." **(James 5:16).**

This is a responsibility of the Christ's church because we have the true Light **(Is. 60:1).** We have the answers that the world needs, and we have to live it as we come into understanding our role as wives and be willing to give it to others who are in darkness and have no hope.

In my ministry of teaching, sharing and learning with other women, my heart just cries as I think of so many precious women of God who desperately need loving spiritual mothers and sisters to come to them while there is hope. Because they don't, relationships and families lie in ruins only to have to same problems repeat because we do not give attention to God's word on marriage to obey.

This manner of conduct you cannot fake. You cannot be one way when you're out in public settings representing your family and then another way when you are at home. Your family, your husband will see right through it.

Calling Him "Lord"

It's called hypocrisy, and you'll lose your witness and the influence that you have as a woman.

Jesus' Sermon on the Mount **Matthew 5–7** is very encouraging to bring us back to the right heart attitude and faith response. For years now, it has represented a refreshing place to retreat and regroup for me. Attitudes and behaviors are not something you can touch with your hand, but they are displayed all the time and often speak louder than words. They can affect the whole atmosphere.

For example, think about a group of people together enjoying one another, maybe just getting started at work or a game, then someone comes in who is perilous and angry. The person makes biting remarks and threats to others. If the situation is not dealt with wisely, it will affect the whole atmosphere and maybe a fight will break out. However, if that same person comes in angry and argumentative, and a person of integrity with a calm spirit responds in love and grace speaking truth with kindness and respect, he or she can defuse or quench that angry spirit and cause a shift, changing the whole atmosphere in a powerful and positive way. This is what God is saying that we, particularly as women, must be prepared to do.

"She openeth her mouth with wisdom; and in her tongue is the law of kindness" **(Prov. 31:26).**

Story

A couple was arguing and yelling at one another, so much so that the man— frustrated, humiliated and belittled by the woman— in the heat of anger pulls out a gun. He approaches to shoot her when a *4-foot 9*-inch woman who was also present stands between the two, facing him, looks him in the eye and gently says, *"Now you don't want to do that."* The man, towering over this little woman, begins to cry. Fortunately, he does not carry out what could have been a tragic act. The desire of the devil to kill was stopped. The spirit of anger and rage was broken, diffused.

Thank God! Now, what was it about the act of this quiet little woman? It wasn't that she in herself was so strong but that she was adorned or clothed with a meek and quiet spirit (1 Peter 3:4). It was the precious Spirit of Jesus, the Holy Spirit, who was working through this woman. This is a true story, and that woman was my mother whom I observed for years. From her, I learned to serve and love my husband as she did my father.

Sadly, all stories do not have such fortunate endings. On another occasion, a couple was visiting at our home and the women ended up stabbing her husband who had been known to abuse her. He died there in our home.

You see, there's a real need for work on marital relationships and a serious work that is worthy of our utmost attention. You may have a network in your neighborhood of men and women who have developed friendship relationships of teaching, sharing and mentoring. If so, that's a good thing, but I think it should also be a purposeful, targeted, more intentional area of ministry through the church as well.

We have to pray and gear up to respond strategically, forcefully and effectively because of the troublesome times in which we live.

"Thou shalt keep them, O Lord, thou shalt preserve them from this generation forever. The wicked walk on every side, when the vilest men are exalted" (**Ps. 12:7-8**).

Our laws are changing, bringing ungodly movements, corrupt leaders, launching a direct attack on marriages from the original foundation and intent. We can certainly be sure of this, that the God of our Lord Jesus Christ can and will make a distinction between His own and the world in the end.

"Then shall ye return, and discern between the righteous and the wicked, between him that serveth God and him that serveth him not" (**Mal. 3:18**).

It's Time to Rise Up Women of God, The Night Is Far Spent

"That the aged men be sober, grave, temperate, sound in faith, in charity, in patience. The aged women likewise, that they be in behaviour as becometh holiness, not false accusers, not given to much wine, teachers of good things; That they may teach the young women to be sober, to love their husbands, to love their children. To be discreet, chaste, keepers at home, good, obedient to their own husbands, that the word of God be not blasphemed"(**Tit. 2:2-5**).

The Contrast: Vashti and Esther

"A virtuous woman is a crown to her husband: but she that maketh ashamed is as rottenness in his bones" (**Prov. 12:4**).

Take Queen Vashti for example:
"But the queen Vashti refused to come at the king's commandment by his chamberlains: therefore was the king very wroth, and his anger burned in him. Then the king said to the wise men... What shall we do unto the queen Vashti according to law, because she hath not performed the commandment of the king Ahasuerus by the chamberlains? And Memucan answered before the king and the princes, Vashti the queen hath not done wrong to the king only, but also to all the princes, and to all the people that are in all the provinces of the king Ahasuerus. For this deed of the queen shall come abroad unto all women, so that they shall despise their husbands in their eyes, when it shall be reported, The king Ahasuerus commanded Vashti the queen to be brought in before him, but she came not. Likewise shall the ladies of Persia and Media say this day unto all the king's princes, which have heard of the deed of the queen. Thus shall there arise too much contempt and wrath (**Es. 1:12-18**).

I have heard a lot expressed regarding Vashti, justifying her position in doing what she did, but the bottom line is she lost out because of it.

Unlike Vashti, Esther, though chosen to be queen, always honored the king showing such reverence. Take note of how she addresses him, regarding the banquet to which she wishes to summon Haman:

"And Esther answered, if it seems good unto the king..."(**Es. 5:4**)."
Look at how the king responds:
"Then the king said, Cause Haman to make haste, that he may do as Esther hath said.... "(**Es. 5:5**).

Again she addresses the king:

"If I have found favor in the sight of the king, and if it please the king to grant my petition, and to perform my request, let the king and Haman come to the banquet that I shall prepare for them, and I will do tomorrow as the king hath said **(Es. 5:8).**

The Book of Esther includes other examples where she refers to the king in this gentle manner.

It is quite clear, Esther called her husband "the king," "lord." She came before the king when it could have cost her life, and she continued even after to address him with the same respect. Vashti, on the other hand, was properly sent for, didn't show up and ridiculed the king, suffering the consequences.

I know this is not going to sit well with some. It didn't with me at first. God told me I had to decrease **(Jn. 3:30),** I had to die to myself. Remember, the virtuous woman is a rare find, but stands out among many as Esther did, and the Bible gives us other examples: Ruth, Abigail, Manoah's wife, Sarah, Hannah; So, though virtuous women are rare **(Prov. 31:10),** you will not be alone.

So we can conclude that the foolish woman who tears her house down, mainly does so by what she says and how she says it. Her speech and manner shows or displays dishonor **(Prov. 14:1).**

I conclude with this, as we decrease and allow God to increase **(Jn. 3:30)** serving and honoring our own husbands, calling them lords, we'll give the Lord opportunity to show Himself mighty in our lives and circumstances. I'm not saying this is easy, because the flesh dies hard and this will look different for each one of us. The bottom line is, it's not about us. It is about Jesus Christ, and that's a good thing. When we embrace these truths and obey God, then we will experience our destiny unfolding and the destinies of others. God will be pleased because He will be glorified. Finally, realize this, and please excuse my vernacular, but, *"Ain't nobody mad but the devil!"*

So, like Sarah to whom we are to look, those of us who seek the *Lord,* His righteousness **(Is. 51:1-2),** like Esther and other rare virtuous women we know today, I yield in submission to God, and in that, I chose then and still choose today, *to call him lord. To God Be the Glory!*

About The Author

Born to Tom and Blanche Fuller in June 1960 as Linda Michele, I was a very shy, withdrawn person resulting from trauma early on from a tragic house fire that took the life of my older toddler sister, Gwen. Even as a baby, I was familiar with grief and sadness that seemed to cloak our household and family. Later, coming to the saving knowledge of Jesus Christ, I discov- ered the gift of wisdom that God was operating in my life.

I was encouraged to journal and was very thankful to have such a release of so much knowledge and understanding. Many years later another house fire took the life of my loving father age 82, not long after he stood to give me away as I transitioned from daughter to wife. My *Isaiah 6:1-8* experience at that time brought me to another level in the Lord and I felt inspired to write. This book is the second title I felt God dropped into my spirit.

Six months before my father's passing, I received a profound call to worship. Through the Spirit, I was led to an open door for teaching, leading worship and overseeing two worship teams.

In 1995, I was given the opportunity to lead one of the church cell groups to share with other women from my own journey in learning how to submit to God's plan, His individual design for each person and His or- der for living a fulfilled life. Later, after relocating, I was able to share in a care group at our church in Philadelphia, then on to a home Bible study and prayer crisis ministry focused on family and marriage.

I was ordained a preacher in 1998 at Pentecostal Assembly of Jesus Christ in North Carolina, but a sudden relocation and tumultuous turn of events threatened to rip apart and destroy our beautiful marriage and fam- ily. This led me underground for a time into a place of focused intercession and strategy of the Lord (principles of submission to pursue what the enemy Satan had lied about, stolen and ravaged but could not destroy because of the Mighty hand of God.

Here God was allowing an opportunity for me to see at work His wis-dom and power through submission, trusting Him and His exploits of answered prayer and intervention. So now God's leading has reestablished our family in Wilmington, Delaware and directed me back to the journals and writings to finish this book

Since 2008, I've been blessed with the opportunity to attend Elim Bi-ble Institute for biblical studies and join the fellowship at RWO *(Restoration World Outreach)* for much-needed prophetic training and activation for preparation at this set timing of favor, breakthroughs, fulfillment and fruitfulness in my life personally as well as being a very functional working part for the Body of Christ.

I'm excited to share this unbiased view God has given me on submis-sion to Him particularly as a wife, yet also wherever I am and in whatever role I find myself as He has released me to destiny and being a vessel of honor to Him, also releasing others to restoration and destiny. All for His Glory!

Under The Leadership of Pastors Tom and Barbara Davis

REFERENCES

Barlow, Omar Rev. (2008-2009), New Year's Message "Before" (Recorded by New Covenant Church). Philadelphia, PA:

Dictionary Word Definition . Retrieved from http://dictionary .reference.com/

Handford, Elizabeth Rice (1994). Me Obey him? (Sword of the Lord Publishers) Revised Edition

King James Version of the Holy Bible

You Are LOVED Holy Bible, Second Edition (October 2007). Holy Bible New Living Translation, (1996, 2004, 2007) by Tyndale House Foundation Inc. Carol

Stream, IL

All rights reserved

WARERESOURCES AND PUBLISHING
WE ARE AN ALL IN ONE,
ONE STOP PUBLISHING COMPANY!!!!

W.R.P. is a modest but skillful and knowledgeable Christian Publishing Company. We specialize in getting authors into print. We embrace and guide each author like a member of our family. We treat you fairly and recognize the importance of building a lasting relationship with you as an author. Join us in the walk to promote prosperity along with the message of encouragement and peace. Be one of the authors we transform and prepare for the world of information and books.

FEEL FREE TO CONTACT US@
www.wareresources.com
1-800-469-4850 EXT. 2

CPSIA information can be obtained
at www.ICGtesting.com
Printed in the USA
LVOW13s0036270318
571269LV00032B/446/P